French Girl
Rendez-vous

Laure Danglade

French Girl Rendez-vous

A Novel

PGCOM Éditions

Table

A Richard et Honorine

Toujours aller de l'avant [1]

"If we knew what was going to happen, life wouldn't be as fun," my grandmother used to tell me when I got impatient. She was right. But some days you would give anything to know what's coming. When I boarded this plane from Paris to Boston, I would have given anything for a sign—just to make sure I was doing the right thing. I was so happy to leave my country and the boring life I had there to become an American student! At the same time, I was scared, not really knowing what to expect… and I had such huge expectations!

I remember my tense feeling in the airport customs line. I wanted to leave. I was ready to explode.

Today, 3 years later, I would tell myself, "Slow down, you are so lucky. Enjoy every step." Well, I confess that during the first few weeks after my arrival in Massachusetts I wanted to go back home several times! But, as the Americans say, *"Hang in there, it's gonna be ok."*

1 Always move forward

1. *J'y suis* [1]

I am waiting my turn in line. I hold on tightly to the papers in my right hand. At least 7 people are ahead of me. I check and organize all of my documents. In order: my passport opened to my F1 Visa page, my DS2019 from the American Embassy in Paris, all of the papers from the university I am to attend, and, like everyone else, the little green immigration paper they give you on the plane. It all has to be in order. I tell myself that this paperwork will allow me to easily enter the U.S. I used colorful stickers to classify each document type. It will be fine. I am in the Non-Resident Immigration arrival line at the Boston airport. I have endured months of bureaucratic paperwork to get here. If one signature, stamp, or certificate is missing, "too bad," they'll tell me, "you'll have to try another time," and then send me back home. Even though I have checked my paperwork a hundred times, I can't help but be scared of the immigration official at the desk. I am almost there. No way they'll send me back to Paris.

In the line across from me, a girl, a brunette my age is struggling with her bag. It is huge and shapeless. How could she take this thing as a carry-on? She pushes it with her feet each time her line moves, and this amuses a very tall guy behind her. He keeps his hands in his pockets, and I can see his immigration paperwork, neatly organized in the inside pocket of his jacket.

My line moves, and 2 people approach the immigration desk. The expressionless official checks their passport and talks to them, then takes their fingerprints and lets them pass. It seems easy from a distance. And it's my turn.

---

1 I made it

After a short pause, I manage to put my right foot in front of my left foot and move toward the plastic cage that contains the official. With my head straight and a smile on my lips, I walk up to the desk. It might seem silly, but I'm scared. The official looks like a policeman. Maybe he is. He looks at me and frowns. I smile. I put my left hand on a green machine and my fingerprints are captured. Then my right hand. He asks me to look at the webcam. Is he going to scan my retina like in a James Bond movie? No, he just took a picture. Then he concentrates on my papers. They all are in the correct order. I relax my shoulders. Then he stares at me:
"What are you going to do in Boston?"
"Heu je…I…I will…"
I am not sure what to say. Words aren't coming out of my mouth. I don't panic. I smile. Then he shows me a document from the university:
"You're going to study at the university, right?"
"Yes! University. I learn English."
It is the first sentence I've spoken to a real American guy. I smile. He looks me over and is not impressed. Then he takes my airline ticket and asks:
"This is your return ticket?"
"Return, yes!"
Then it was his turn to smile! I now wonder what would have happened if he had known that I never took this flight home? Today, neither of us knows this. He grabs a stapler and click! He seals my destiny with a "good to go!"
My heart beats like crazy. I know I will never be the same person when I return to France. I come from a small, quiet city in Normandy where nothing ever happens. Now I'm becoming an American student like the ones I watch in my favorite TV shows. I would like to freeze everything that I think I know and capture it, because I know it's going to change.
"Next, please!"
The officer rustles me from my daydream. He waves up the next passenger. I have to go. Well, that was easy.

I pass through the door to the luggage area like one crosses the finish line of a marathon. I find my way to the baggage claim like I am surfing on a cloud. A female voice that I don't understand spews from a speaker. *Oui*, I don't speak English. Moving to country in which you do not speak the language sounds fun, no? Not everyone speaks English in France. Anyway, I am looking at my bags but there are so many people around me. My head meets the others' shoulders. I'm 5 feet tall on a good day. That's short—even in France. I catch a glimpse of my bags, and I pounce for them. I love my Longchamps bag. Having one is a must in Normandy.

Thankfully, 'taxi' is the same in French. I scan the handwritten signs the drivers are holding for my name. Nobody is waiting for me. I don't know anyone on this continent. And that's why I am here. "Total immersion in an English speaking country is the best way to learn the language"-- that's what they say. Well, I worked for less than a year in Paris and discovered that not being bilingual is a disadvantage. I have always been a bad student in foreign languages. *Oh oui*, 'speak fluent English' is a magic phrase in France! There are even ads in the subway.

The upcoming six months are going to be intense. Only six months to learn English in a program through an American University that immerses students in the American way of life. USA *voilà*!

My eyes re-read a sign held by one of the taxi drivers. "Auralee Gourdan." It sounds vaguely familiar.

"*Oh ! C'est moi!* This is me!" I exclaim.

My name is Aurélie Jourdan. I realize that my first mistake occurred before I even set foot on American soil. I misspelled my name when I booked the taxi. In French, the letter "J" is pronounced like the letter "G" in English. Likewise, the letter "I" is pronounced like the letter "E." And Americans don't use accents!

The driver stares at me with a playful look, so I smile and he tries: "Miss O-a-l-ee?"

I realize that my name is not easy for Americans to say, and hope for the future that it is not impossible.

"Good afternoon, sir!" My answer makes him laugh. He asks:

"Blah blah blah… France? Blah blah blah."
"Oui, France!"
I don't understand him, but I know what to do! I silently thank my mother for the little pink card she made me with the name and the address of the school I am going to. The driver looks at it and seems to understand where I would like to go. Great, that makes one of us, I think.

In the back of the cab, I open my window. I am filled with energy. I want to enjoy every moment. I want to have fun all the time. I have a good feeling. Coming to Boston was a good choice. I am happy with my decision!
The University I am going to is in Newton, not far from Boston. I am impressed by the landscape. So many hills and huge trees… nothing like Normandy, where we have only grass and apple trees. Normandy is like England--always grey and rainy. The only difference is that Normands don't speak English.
I have to resolve this language barrier. Being a journalist in Paris could have been fun if I had known how to speak English. In Paris, many symposiums are held in English. Although I had studied English in school, to my surprise, I didn't understand a word of the first conference I covered on the "image" of chemistry. The other journalists did. I have to learn to speak English fluently. That's why I am in this cab. I am more than happy to be a student again and, in particular, an American student!

*

The cab drops me in front of a mansion at 749 East Ave, Newton, Massachusetts. A beautiful bay window catches my attention; we don't have these type of windows in France. I walk up the few steps and enter.
Laughter. It's what I hear first. People are laughing to my left. The mansion is full of life. A group of Asian students is playing Pictionary in the classroom to my left. To my right, I see an open door labeled "Office of the Director," and I gather that I am standing in

front of the administrative assistant's desk. Several pretty, sophisti-cated girls are reclining on a couch near the coffee machine. They stare at me for a second and go back to their cheerful conversation. I think they are speaking Spanish? I catch a glimpse of the stairs leading to classrooms.

"Blah blah blah?"

I hear a voice. Someone is talking to me. It's coming from the guy seated at the desk. He gestures toward me, so I follow him and smile.

"Good afternoon, Sir. My name is Aurélie."

"Hi! I'm Jack! I'm the blah blah blah..."

Though he is clearly making an effort to speak very slowly and articulate, I have no clue what he is saying. I get the impression he wants me to sit down, so I do.

"Take a seat! Please! Give me your papers and I'll show you around."

I smile. He keeps talking. I don't understand a word, and I feel terrible just letting him talk and talk... I end up confessing:

"Jack, I don't understand! I am sorry..."

"That's fine! It's how you'll learn. You'll pick up a few words until eventually you get the whole sentence!"

He is nice. Good point, I think to myself. I give him my registra-tion papers--meaning I open my bag and give him every paper in sight. He takes certain papers, returns the rest, nods, and says a cheerful "welcome!" Jack stands up, so I stand up. He walks, so I walk behind him. We go outside. He gives me a tour of the cam-pus. It's huge, it's beautiful, it's the U.S.! And Jack is the same: he's huge, he's beautiful, he's American.

"Over there is the cafeteria, behind it is the gym, and on this side, the library."

The campus looks exactly as I pictured a British college would look--an old dormitory. All of the foreign students live in the same building, but we share the library, the cafeteria, the gym, and the baseball field with the American students.

Right in the middle of the campus, Jack stops in the front of a five-story building.

"This is it. Your room is 102B, ok? Class starts tomorrow at blah blah blah, ok?"
"Thank you very much Jack!" I manage to say.
I don't really understand, but with the time difference, I won't be late tomorrow! And, luckily, my room number is written on the keychain.

My room is symmetric - a one-person bed against the wall, a wardrobe, and a desk under two windows. The building is composed of six-person apartments, two each to a room. The six of us share the living room (with the TV) and the kitchen. With six women sharing this living space, I am glad to see that there are two bathrooms!
My roommate arrived a few days ago, Jack tells me. I am excited to meet the girl I'm going to share the next six months of my life with. I've never had a roommate before. I begin to unpack and arrange my things. It's only 6 p.m., but I'm exhausted. I fall into my bed. I imagine what will happen tomorrow, all the people I'll meet. I can't wait to make friends from all over the world.

My head is heavy, and my neck hurts. It's six hours earlier here than in France, so it has been a long day for me. I close my eyes in the darkness of the room. I wonder if my roommate is coming soon. I'd like to give her a good first impression. I'll wake up anyway when she gets back. It's such a great feeling to finally relax.
I dream of all the places I've ever hoped to visit that are now so close... I wonder how it feels to think in another language... I can see myself Skyping with my French friends. They ask, "what are you doing this weekend?" And I reply, "I don't know, I'll probably go to New York, you know, do some shopping on 5th Avenue — you know, normal American stuff."
It'll be so cool! New York, it's just a four-hour drive. Anyway, I hope I'll make good friends and meet interesting people...I hope everyone will be nice...I mean, I hope I'll meet some great guys... I mean, I hope I'll meet *the* guy! I'd love to have an American boyfriend. Why not?

I'm 24. I'm single. I've never been lucky with men. I always meet *'boulet.'* *'Boulet'* is the French word my girlfriends and I use for guys who end up breaking our hearts. To translate it, a *'boulet'* in French would be the ball in the saying 'ball and chain.' But I've figured out my mistake: wrong country! Looking for a guy in France, what a foolish idea! The man of my life lives here, in the U.S. That's why we haven't met yet. He is waiting for me here. It's my first night on American soil, and I want him to hear my call, "I'm coming, my love!"

I picture him, my American boyfriend. He is handsome like Chuck in *Gossip Girl*. Or cool like Joey in *Friends*, and he says, "How you doin'?" and wink at me.

Obviously, he will immediately fall for my French accent. He will eventually learn French, of course, and we will split our lives between Boston and Paris, and our children will have two native languages. It will be such a wonderful life… We will live happily ever after.

Am I asking too much? No way… My mom has a friend who knows a woman whose daughter did a summer internship in Chicago and came back with an American husband. See, it can happen. I have proof. And now, it's my turn. When I think of it, it seems so obvious: the first guy I kissed was American. I met him during an exchange students' program in high school. I've known it from the beginning. It's an American boyfriend I need.

2. *Où est mon atlas?* [1]

8h45. I mean 8:45 a.m. Class starts in 15 minutes. I wake up. It's hard to leave the arms of my American boyfriend …Damn it, it was just a dream… But I get out of bed to make it come true. Wake up! Wake up! Wake up! I run to the bathroom. I put on a cute black skirt. I'm a perfect student. I notice that there is still no sign of my roommate. She didn't come in last night. Hopefully I'll meet her in class.

I'm early! I love living so close to the classroom. In France, college isn't laid out like that. We don't have "campuses"—no little 'college towns,' with everything a student could need! In France, universities don't usually have dormitories right next to the buildings in which classes are held. Students usually find an apartment in town and commute to classes daily. Everything here is so close!

I find my way to the right classroom. The room is cozy. Thanks to my seat, I already feel like an American student. The classroom has those individual attached wooden desks that you enter from the side. A world map hangs on the wall in the front of the classroom. Of course, I eye France. It's 9 a.m. on the dot. A tall, fit, middle-aged woman enters. She goes directly to the board and puts her hands on her hips and smiles, looking around the room. The classroom quiets. It must be a universal reflex when the teacher comes in. I bet, like me, she is wondering where we are from.

The young guy sitting next to me seems very tall. I can tell he is not comfortable in his desk. His arms and legs hang over and out of his desk, making him look like a giant--like the scene in *Alice in Wonderland* where Alice's head goes through the roof of the mushroom house. The poor guy extends his legs in every direction, trying to

1 Where is my atlas ?

21

find a comfortable position... He has Asian eyes and a snow-white complexion. Korean maybe? The girl sitting directly in front of me has long, beautiful, shiny blond hair like in a magazine ad. This girl is lucky, I think. Her dark skin stands in beautiful contrast to her light hair. I have no clue where she is from, either.

And what about me? Do I look French? Are they looking at me, thinking, "Oh, she's French." I've never really thought about this before. In France, I am the easy-going Aurélie, with the same boring Normandy life ...

I am a small, freckled brunette. Do I look French? At this moment I feel the weight of all French civilization on my shoulders. Am I a good representative of my country? Are there some rules to being a French girl that I am not aware of? I have no idea where the other students are from. What do they think of me?

The teacher, Miss McCarty, ends my little guessing game. She asks us to write down our first name and where we are from on a piece of paper and place it on our little desk. The easy way. I am disappointed.

Well, I have some good guesses and some bad guesses as to the origin of my classmates. The guy with the snow-white skin and Asian eyes is Taras, from Kazakhstan. It's tough to locate on the map hanging at the front of the classroom, and I'm confused. The pretty girl is Claudia, pronounced Cla-o-dia, from Brazil. She could pass as Gisele Bundchen's sister. So unfair. And there is Hyun Jung, a Korean girl. There is Manuel, also from Brazil, with curly hair. I can picture him in a swimsuit on a beach named "cabana-something." Brazil seems like a nice country. I have to visit it someday. Then there is Kenji from Japan. I knew it. He is stylish, fit, and smart-looking, my exact perception of a typical Japanese guy. Near him is Niran from Thailand, who doesn't really look Asian. And finally there is Sofia from Italy. She seems younger than the rest of us. We all look to be about 25, but Sofia is 18. We're all here to learn English. Our common goal--isn't it exciting!

Back in my room that evening, I check out each of my classmates' countries on the Internet. I learn that Thailand has a king. Kazakhstan's capital is Astana, and it is between China and Russia, which explains Taras' white skin and Chinese eyes. I feel pretty bad about my lack of world knowledge. How can I expect people to know my country if I don't know anything about theirs? I go to bed. I haven't spoken French all today, not even a word. I have a headache. And where is my roommate?

*

"Shhhhhhhhhhhh!" Giggling sounds fill my room. "Shhhhhhhhh!" I open my eyes to darkness.
"Slow down," says a female voice.
"No!" says a male voice.
"My roommate is here, she's probably sleeping!"
"Come on!"
Am I still dreaming? What's going on? I hear more giggling. Then I can smell... blecchh! The late-night smell of sweat, beers and cigarettes envelop the room... When it's your smell, it's often exciting. When it's others' smell, it's disgusting. I can't believe it. I hear a 'bang.' Not just any kind of 'bang', the bang of two bodies hitting a bed. And more giggling. *Bien sûr!* Of course! This is not happening. Heavy breathing sounds, sheets moving... They're having sex. I cover my head with my pillow. What should I do? Should I turn on the light? How can they do this, knowing I'm here? Come on! This must be a joke. "Please stop," I think to myself... I wish I could teleport myself anywhere but here. Who does this? Am I the only one who thinks this is inappropriate? No way.
The noises quiet pretty quickly. Good for me. And I hear the door slamming. Now, I'm not so much looking forward to meeting my roommate. I never thought we would become so intimate so quickly.

*

The first thing I see when I open my eyes in the morning is a very young and pretty girl dancing around and singing in front of her wardrobe. She is glowing with happiness. Is she kidding me? She realizes I am awake and says:

"Hi! I'm Kristina from Venezuela!"

"*Bonjour*…I mean hi! I am Aurélie."

"Aurrrrélie! Where are you from?" She says my name in such a beautiful way, the opposite the American pronunciation.

"I'm from France."

"No way! Paris! So cool!"

"Well… Thank you…"

"And how old are you?"

"*Je*… I am…" I am still shocked from her behavior last night and trying to wake up, so it's hard for me to speak English…

"I am 18 and I love to party. And you?" she says.

That's so great! Lucky me… She is dancing like a butterfly in front of her wardrobe, in tiny shorts with something written on the bottom. I have never seen these kinds of shorts before. She is acting like nothing happened last night.

I feel like I've aged 5 years in one second. I consider myself an 'in' person. I go to popular nightclubs in Paris (ok, once). I am very fashionable (I have one designer dress, but I never wear it for fear of damaging it). I have lots of fun friends (this one is true!). And most importantly, I feel like an 18 year old (at heart).

But today I can't compete.

*

I stop by Jack's office on my way to class. I prepared for my conversation with him with what would become my new best friend: my Harrap's dictionary. I ask:

"Hi Jack! Could I exchange my roommate?"

He laughs and, after a moment, says:

"Excuse me?"

I had only prepared that one sentence, so I repeat:

"Hi Jack! Could I exchange my roommate?"

"What's going on?"

He seems embarrassed by my question. Now I have to improvise:

"She lives during the night and I live during the day." I am not sure this sentence is correct, but I have to say something.

24

"Okay…"

Does he understand? Who knows? He looks at his computer and says:

"Done! I put you with Yuriko—she's Japanese and your age, ok?"

"Thank you very much, Sir Jack."

That was so easy. My English is so good already! I can solve any problem! I keep smiling at Jack, as if he were the king of the world. He notices how relieved I am and adds:

"You're cute. I like blah blah blah! There are not many French students here!"

I wish I understood. I blush a little, but I can't respond… So I nod…

Today in grammar class it's hard to concentrate… I have a second chance in the roommate department. I am so glad. The day goes quickly and I find myself packing again! I feel a bit anxious. What if the new roommate is worse than the current one? Is that even possible?

So here I am, standing in front of room 205B. I noticed Jack said 'two 'o five B.' Isn't it 'two hundred and five B?' This must be why I didn't understand him the last time he gave me a number. I have to adjust this "o" versus "0" way of saying numbers! I knock and open the door.

"Hi!" I say loudly—I know how to make an entrance! The girl jumps up from her computer chair.

"Hi! Sorry I startled you. I'm Aurélie. Your new roommate. Nice to meet you!"

She stands up and joins me. She is the cutest thing ever, nothing like the excited, cheerleader-like Venezuelan. I have a good feeling about Yuriko. She wears her dark black hair in a bob. It fits her round face well. She is just as petite as me, and I like her style. Her T-shirt is fashionable—very original, with a big flower pin. She's wearing those jeans with a paint splash on them that are so popular right now.

Without speaking, she invites me to come in by gesturing to what will be my side of the room.

25

"Thank you!" I say, putting my luggage on my bed.

"You're welcome," she replies.

She stares at me. I stare at her. We don't have the words, but I feel like we would say important things if we could. It's the thought that counts, right? She is trying to say something, but can't quite get it out. I'm motivated to learn to communicate with her, which will be good practice for talking to my future American boyfriend. She continues to stare at me as I unpack. Finally, she says:

"My name is Yuriko. I am from Tokyo, Japan... I am 24 years old...I studied science...I am happy to meet you." Then she sighed and shrugged her shoulders. I can't help but notice that it sounds like something she learned by heart and repeated in one breath. It's so touching. I understand the effort and appreciate it.

We smile. I walk over to her desk to look at the many photos she has on the wall. She points to each one. 'Family,' 'friends...' She is eager to show me one specific heart-framed picture. I recognize her in the arms of a guy. 'Boyfriend,' she says, and adds: "his name is Kenta, he is in Japan." She has a genuinely sad look on her face...

I don't know what to say, but my Latin roots lead me to place my hand on her arm to comfort her, to show her I understand. She recoils. *Oh mon Dieu,* Oh my God! That was not a good idea. *Ou la la,* she seems so scared and troubled! "Sorry so sorry, *je suis désolée*..." I say. Finally, she laughs, so I laugh too. Our first cultural misunderstanding! I knew I would encounter some cultural misunderstandings here, but I really don't know what to do...

"That's ok. No problem." She says after a moment evaluating the situation. "I need to remember not to touch Asian people," I think. Then she asks:

"And you? Boyfriend?" Ouch!

"No. I am single."

Now it's her turn to look at me with sadness. I wonder if "*Catherinette* day" exists in Japan. It's a fun tradition in France – depending on which side you're on. If you're single when you turn 25, your girlfriends give you a hat that you have to wear all day, so everyone knows you're still single. It's mostly fun for everyone else.

26

Well, her boyfriend is in Japan. Tough for her, but good for me. He won't stop by at night, and for that I am very glad. So, after getting to know my new roommate, I direct the conversation to a common international girls' interest: *la mode*, fashion! I ask her to follow me, and we compare our clothes and accessories. We laugh a lot. I am surprised to see that her wardrobe is a mess despite her meticulously maintained desk. She has a lot of clothes.

When we turn off the lights and prepare for bed, I'm so happy. I have a Japanese friend! It's cool—exactly what I wanted. I am already living an amazing life.

Now that I am settled and feel good, it's time to let my *poulettes*, the little nickname I have for my girlfriends Caroline, Stéphanie, Manue and Clémence, know I've arrived and I'm doing well!

From: LapetiteAurélieUSA
To: *"Poulettes"*
Subject: The package has been delivered

Salut! (Hi! In French)

Everything is going well.
No I haven't met my American boyfriend yet, and the guy who sat next to me on the plane wasn't cute.
The campus is huge. There's a baseball field, a gym complex, and a cafeteria where I can get peanut butter at any time of day.
My roommate is Japanese, my same age, and she loves shopping: we're going to get along.
I learned a new word—"awesome." Everything is awesome here, apparently. lol

I already miss you,
Aurélie, ready to conquer the USA!

3. Dans la peau d'une étudiante Américaine [1]

Spending the day in an American student's shoes is awesome. Maybe I love it because I know what it's like to cycle between home, the office, home, bed, the office, home… etc. I have to say, student life is better, and the American student life is more than better! *C'est le top!* It's the best!

My classes are great. I eat burgers for lunch with my classmates from all over the world. French people tend to say that burgers aren't good, but damn they are! I go back to class in the afternoon, but only until 3 p.m. After that, it's gym time, but I pass on that and go shopping on Newberry Street with Yuriko. I explore the city with an English guidebook. I go to Boston Common and sit on a bench where I feed pieces of my muffin to the squirrels, such cute little creatures. I have never seen so many so close up. Downtown Boston is very European, with its architecture, and non-parallel streets. I feel so good here. Jack told me that last year they had a lot of trouble with a homesick Taiwanese girl. I, on the contrary, feel better than ever here.

My classes are so much fun—like none that I've ever had before. And I'm not bad in school here. My English skills are improving pretty quickly. Miss McCarty, *la professeur*, the professor, encourages us to watch TV and go to the movie theater. Every Monday, she shows us *Cold Case Files*, a police show that takes place in Philadelphia. I have never heard of this city, but it seems dangerous. She records the show every week and we spend the first two classes on it. Sometimes we watch the news, which is harder for me because the speaker doesn't speak clearly. Is this a game? How do they understand each other? I have to figure this out.

1 In an American student's shoes

Bref, anyway, the main character of *Cold Case Files* is Lilly Rush. Every Monday Miss McCarty welcomes us with a cheerful "it's Lilly Rush time!" And it's during one of these Monday sessions that she nicknamed me 'Lilly.'

Ok, Aurélie is impossible to say if the 'r' sound doesn't exist your language. My classmates prefer Lilly too, so everyone is glad that Miss McCarty has nicknamed me. And from now on, no one's throat will hurt when they try to get my attention. I tell myself that to be part of this community, I have to accept this new name. It could have been worse.

Oh oui, as a perfect student, I enjoy going to the library—but not the campus one. I take the 'T' (the name of the subway here) to Coplay Station, where the Boston Public Library is located. The main room is as big as the international arrivals hall at the Paris Charles de Gaulle airport.

There are 2 rows of 20 dark wood tables. At least 10 people can sit across from each other at one table. It reminds me of the main room of the school in *Harry Potter.* But the ceiling isn't a magical sky—it's just a painting.

The pastel colors of these paintings create a romantic atmosphere in contrast to the dark wooden shelves and tables. The shelves are built into all four walls, and you are encircled by authentic 18th century book collections. I had to ask about these books because I had no idea they had an 18th century in the U.S. We Europeans always hear that Americans 'don't have history!'

Bref, when I tap my pen on the table, it makes a metallic cling that reverberates through the room. My neighbors, who I have clearly bothered, stare at me. So I continue doing it, hoping my eyes will cross those of my future American boyfriend. Nothing yet, so I blush and try to hide behind my computer. I'm embarrassed to have interrupted the purring silence that embraces everyone here.

I always sit at the end of the table near the shelves so I can smell the sugary taste of old books.

Practicing my English here makes me feel special. It's nothing like working at the very modern Beaubourg Library in Paris, where the tables are plastic and the colors are flashy. At the Boston Public Library, I can hear the whispers of the old books commenting on visitors' work. They have seen generations and generations of students and others coming here to read, to work, to study. They would have a great story to tell. And now they see us with our computers…I am sure that makes a 200-year-old book crazy.

The most enjoyable thing about working in this library is, for me, playing with the adorable little green lamps. There are 5 at the center of each table, each with a little gold string hanging from the lampshade. I love playing with it! I really feel like an American student here.

*

One thing I enjoy that I shouldn't here is the food. *Ou la la! La cuisine* in the U.S. is so good. We all go for breakfast, lunch and dinner to this wonderful place called "the cafeteria." The only problem is that dinner is served between 5 p.m. and 6 p.m. I can only imagine the Spanish people's frustration.

For breakfast, no *croissant* but pancakes, or, even more bizarre, salty food: eggs and sausage. I just can't! Maybe with time I will appreciate it. One thing I love: bagels with cream cheese. Ok, *fromage*, cheese, as we call it in France, is very far from this smooth, silky white cream, but it's tasty. And to replace my *Nutella*, the best ever chocolate mixture for toast, I use peanut butter. I love peanut butter. And the best peanut butter concoction was created by an American—it's called a Reese's Peanut Butter Cup.

Ok, if we keep this up, Yuriko and I will be obese by spring semester. We don't want to be that much a part of the American culture, so we bought a rice cooker. One portion of rice for dinner will make up for our huge breakfast and lunch, we reason.

At the apartment we get along well with the two Korean girls, with whom we share the suite, including Hyun Jung, who is in class with me. I notice that the hardest thing to share when you live in an international environment is the fridge! Food is *the* thing that separates us the most. What do Koreans eat with every meal? Kimchee.

And what is Kimchee? It's cabbage marinated in hot pepper and ginger sauce. They eat it with every single meal. Every time I open the fridge, I am overcome with a strong spicy odor or the smell of dried fish delicatessen. I know I'll get used to it. I like Kimchee, I do. But for dinner. So, it's still hard every morning when I open the fridge to get my milk.

*

As usual, I check my e-mail every morning before class. Today, an email catches my attention. *Non*, not one from my mom – that would be a miracle. She is against technology. She doesn't have a cell phone and she is not capable of sending an email. How have I not thought about moving abroad before? From the other side of the Atlantic Ocean, I'm free! I keep in touch with family through my brother, who is a computer geek.

But this email is from my former editor-in-chief. I read:

"*Bonjour l'Américaine!*" –Nice…

"Remember how we were trying to partner with the Science History Association in Philadelphia? I told them I had a journalist in the U.S.—you. They will cover the cost of your trip if you write an article for me to publish about a symposium they are organizing.

What do you think? Please call Stan at 215 667 8976.

À bientôt,

Sophie"

"Yes!" I think to myself. I am becoming a reporter/journalist/ worldwide professional who goes where the action is. Because I deserve it! *Oh oui!* I can't pass on this one. I'm coming, Stan!!

I have no clue how to get there, but I am so excited to visit another American city!

*

Learning English is my main goal here but come on, don't be silly, an American student has to party! It's part of discovering a culture.

32

And soon it will be Halloween. It's *the* party of the month. Halloween is huge here! I am not worried about going to the unfamiliar city where Lilly Rush fights criminals, but I am so nervous about choosing my Halloween costume. There's a "best costume" prize! Helping to organize the party, I learned that there's a beginning and an end to American parties. *Oui*! I ask Miss McCarty and she explains me that yes, for every kind of event, there's a time to arrive and a time to leave. She seems surprised that I am surprised... I tell her in France you would say 'come at 20h00' (8 p.m.), and people would arrive around 20h30, which is polite. And they don't leave that easily! 'Oh no!' she says. Here, for a barbecue (I learn American people love barbecues), you are invited from 11 a.m. to 6 p.m., or for dinner, from like 6 p.m. to 10 p.m. This is weird to me. I note to myself that, if I meet my American boyfriend at midnight, I have to move fast because he'll need to leave within the hour!??

*

It's the morning of the party. I am all over the place. Tonight, I'll party with the American students. This is such a good opportunity to meet my American boyfriend. Maybe my dream guy is coming tonight.

Things aren't going well on Yuriko's end. I don't speak a word of Japanese, but her last conversation with Kenta sounded more like Goth rock than a love ballad. Usually I enjoy listing to them talking on Skype in the evening, but yesterday I felt uncomfortable and left the room to watch TV. This long distance thing doesn't seem to be working for Yuriko. Sometimes she refuses to go out with us because she's waiting for her Skype *rendez-vous* with him. One cute thing though: Kenta gave her a *Journal*. She writes in it every evening, so he can read it when they see each other again. Very cute. I wonder if a French guy would have thought of something so sweet. Japanese guys seem really great.

From: LapetiteAurélieUSA
To: "*Poulettes*"
Subject: Bad target

Salut!

Comment ca va? I learned the American slang version is, 'How's it goin'?'
The Halloween party was sooooo much fun! My roommate Yuriko won the costume contest. She was a sumo! I helped her blow up her balloon suit!

I flirted with an unknown American soldier...Kidding, it was Jack, the guy I told you about who works at the school office. Anyway, don't celebrate... He told me we definitely have "a thing," —but that he can't. Something about it being against school rules? And he just recently ended a long-term relationship? I didn't really understand what he said, but understood that he is not my American boyfriend. At least I know to focus on someone else.
I needed some cheering up, right? So I ended the evening with Manuel, the cute Brazilian guy... Unfortunately, Brazil was a very disappointing destination.

No comment.
Aurélie

4. *La rencontre* [1]

Here I am on a flight to Philadelphia, in the state of Pennsylvania. It sounds like Transylvania. Maybe I'll meet a sexy vampire? *Bref,* I am so excited—like this is my first interview. Well, it kinda is my first interview—in English. After a 2-hour flight, I arrive in Philadelphia at 2 p.m. I hand the taxi driver the address of the Science History Association.

When I arrive, Stan, the communications manager, has everything under control.

"Bonjour," he welcomes me in a perfect French. I'm impressed. He looks like my old chemistry teacher who I had a crush on.

'I'm Stan. I emailed you. I'm very happy to meet you for this conference.'

'Bonjour.' I say 'I am Aurélie. I am very happy to meet you also.'

I feel welcome and I risk a few polite sayings I learned from Jack. Stan appreciates the effort:

'I am so glad such a great French magazine is covering this event. Your presence is blah blah blah good article, obviously.'

He speaks fast. I smile. He keeps talking:

'The speakers begin at blah blah blah. Your are blah blah at my table for dinner.'

I smile: 'Thank you very much.'

Stan seems very enthusiastic about the article. Should I tell him I don't really understand English? Ok, I'm writing the article in French, but I still have to understand what they're talking about in English...

In the conference room, at least a hundred people are seated to hear 5 speakers debating their views of chemistry today.

The first man stands up and speaks. I hear "blah blah blah...

1 The meeting

[applause]…blah blah blah…[applause]." … *Non!*… What was I thinking? I bite my lips and draw a flower on my notebook… At this moment, my Mitch Buchannan of *Baywatch*, Stan, arrives and whispers in my hear:

'I have the whole conference recorded. I'll have each presentation transcribed and will send them to you, ok?'

Mon héro! My American savior! Stan is such a tactful professional. He saves me the shame of having to admit that I don't understand a word of what's going on.

Oui, when you don't understand a word, time goes very slowly. I have never been so bored at a conference…in my entire natural life. The average age of the crowd around me must be 50. *Ou la la…*

Finally, it's time for dinner! Yes. The moderator asks us to go upstairs. Stan is everywhere, speaking with everyone at dinner except me. This is his job. I smile at my neighbor. He's very old, fat, balding, and ugly. Bad choice on my part. He makes conversation:

'Hi! Sweetie, I noticed you've got an accent. Where are you from?'

'*Bonjour!* My name is Aurélie, I am from France.'

'Of course! Pa-rrrr-is!'

I smile: 'Oui! Paris!'

He stretches his face in an inquisitive way. With one eyebrow up, he says:

'I visited Paris 4 years ago. I remember well. I blah blah blah Saint Michel area. The waiter at the restaurant was awful. Worst blah blah blah ever.'

I understand that something went wrong at a restaurant in Paris. Why is he telling me this? Do I care? He says:

'Don't you think that's ridiculous? Blah blah blah! I was a tourist!'

What should I say? What does he want me to say? Am I responsible for the actions of every French person he has met in his entire life? Come on!

'What happened?' I say politely.

'The waiter blah blah blah. My friend at another table blah blah who can speak few French words blah blah same waiter blah blah adorable!'

What should I say?

'Don't you think he was blah blah impolite! Just because I don't speak French?'

He is getting on my nerves: 'I am so sorry you had a bad service. But you expect from the rest of the world everyone speaks English. Have you tried to say at least '*bonjour*' to this waiter before talking English?'

I am so proud of me. I feel like raising a French flag in victory.

In shock, he replies: 'English is the international language! In every capital of every city in the world, waiters should speak English.'

Ok, being tourist in Paris is tough. But come on! Even with French customers, waiters are horrible! It's the "Parisian style!" *Bref*, this discussion is bothering me. I leave the table.

*

A glass of champagne comforts me at the dessert buffet when I hear a warm voice behind my shoulder: 'Hi! I'm Jeff.'

I face him, and he continues: 'I couldn't help but notice that we are the only 2 people under 30 tonight!'

Oh mon Dieu! He is so close to me, and he is more than good looking. Where was he sitting? How could I have missed him? My heart is aflutter.

'*Bonjour!*' is the only word I can pronounce.

'You're the French journalist, aren't you? First time in Philly?' he says, shaking my hand.

The way he speaks to me is so cute. He articulates well—very thoughtful. He's tall. Well, compared to me, everybody is. But still, he seems tall compared to the others too. He has short, blond hair and blue eyes. He must work out—he's in great shape. His suit is dark brown and compliments his hair color.

"*Oui!* That's me!" I say with a huge smile, not convinced it's the right answer, but hoping it is.

"Would you like to have a drink before you head back to your hotel?"

"*Oui!* I mean, why not? I would enjoy a tour of the city."

Oh mon Dieu! It's happening! To me! A little voice inside me says: 'Do your best. Try to look smart.' Yes! Your American boyfriend is here! Don't blow it!

The good thing about American professional dinner events is that they end early. It's 8 p.m., and it's over! In France, this dinner would begin at 8 p.m.…. *Bref*, I find Stan and thank him. He'll send me the word document, and we'll keep in touch for the article… I take my coat back and meet Jeff outside. I am so happy tonight!

Jeff takes me to a martini bar, The Continental, in the "old city" part of Philadelphia. We talk nonstop. Well, technically he speaks nonstop. I try to understand, and sometimes I even answer. He's cute. When he figures out that I don't understand, he says: 'I'm sorry I talk so fast.' When he gets lost in my English, I say: 'sorry for my French accent,' and he says: 'No! It's cute! Your English is better than my French!'

He's so *adorable.* He's wonderful. I understand that he is finishing his 'P-H-D.' What do these letters stand for? They don't ring a bell, but he seems proud to tell me. Surely he's really smart. He knows Boston, too. He lived there when he was student at MIT. I know what these letter stand for: Massachusetts Institute of Technology. When he says that, I picture him half naked. I know that MIT is a school for geniuses. Then he tells me he will be in Boston soon for an alumni meeting around Thanksgiving. I'll have to look up the word 'alumni,' but does it really matter? It means he'll come to see me soon in Boston. When and what is Thanksgiving? He tells me that this is a holiday celebrated the fourth Thursday of November. I'll have Thursday and Friday off. Nice! In one month!

We tour of the city hand in hand, under the romantic Philadelphia street lights. He walks me back to my hotel, The Omni, at 4th and Chestnut Street. We exchange phone numbers and emails.

"Have a good night!' he says. "*Au revoir!*' The little voice inside me urges me to do something… *Oui*, but what?

'Do you know how we say goodbye in France? We *faire la bise*!' I say.

'Huh? You do what?'

I come very close to him and slowly place a sweet little kiss on his right cheek. He receives it without objection.

'Awesome! You do that every time you say goodbye to anyone?'

'*Oui*! To say 'hi!' and 'bye!' to everyone, yes! And on both cheeks.'

'Interesting . . . '

I came all the way from Normandy for this. My American boyfriend. I can't be shy now. I have to do something.

I close in on his left cheek. As I kiss it, he turns his head, puts his hand in my hair and his lips on my lips. A real kiss. A "French kiss," as the Americans call it. Very long. Very passionate. Very delicate.

I can't remember how to speak English or French. He turns and walks away. He didn't try to coax me into taking him to my room. We have a future together, I think to myself. A wedding? Is he the one? Anyway, we have time, so no need to rush it. Jeff is clearly the perfect American boyfriend I have been looking for. I am head over heels in love with him. I've got an American boyfriend, and it's Jeff!

From: LapetiteAurélieUSA
To: *"Poulettes"*
Subject: *Je le veux !* I do!

Salut!
I found him!!!!!! Yeeeeaaaahhhh! Lol
Not in Boston. I made a longitude-latitude mistake. He is in Phila-
delphia.
I was in the city of brotherly love for an interview—I'll explain
later.
Bref, I met him there! His name is Jeff. He is wonderful. He is my
American boyfriend! I am sooooo happy!
We kissed: *magique*! My first American kiss!
He's 29 and he lives and works in the Philadelphia area. He knows
Boston because he studied at MIT – *Oui*! I love it.
Ok, you're going to say distance is an issue, but not here! Ok, in
France you would not have a boyfriend who lives 4 hours away…
but Americans think differently. They don't care—the country is so
huge!
So distance is not an issue.
He's coming to visit me soon…

On a totally different subject, the other morning I was out with a
Taiwanese girl who was discovering snow! I kid you not, it was the
first time in her life that she had seen snow. It was so much fun!
Even for me it's impressive: the snow is up to my knees. But don't
worry, I will stay warm, thanks to the love of my American boyfriend.

Next time I see him I'll take a picture for you so you can see how
cute he is!
Aurélie, *amoureuse*

5. *Mon film à l'eau de rose* [1]

Back in Boston I tell the whole story to Yuriko. She shares my happiness and we go out to celebrate: shopping on Newberry Street. New boyfriend = new clothes, obviously. Writing to my American boyfriend is a great way to learn English. I spend hours writing to him. It takes me hours to translate his emails, but I do learn a lot of vocabulary.

I also learn a lot by translating the documents Stan sent me to write my French article on the conference. The article is a lot of trouble, but it allowed me to meet Jeff, so I am grateful! *Bref*, I am learning a lot of vocabulary in different fields—in love, and in chemistry.

From: Jeff
To: Aurélie
Subject: Hi!

> *Bonjour Aurelie,*
> *(See, I am speaking French!)*
> *Loved your last email.*
> *Thanksgiving is right around the corner. How about I pick you up on Saturday around 6 p.m.?*
> *Then we'll go to a restaurant in the city. Does the Italian area sound good to you?*
> *I am looking forward to seeing you again.*
> *Jeff.*

Thanks to my Harrap's dictionary I understand that Jeff would like a *rendez-vous* on the Saturday after Thanksgiving, which is celebrated on a Thursday. Nice! What a perfect gentleman! I am so looking

---

1 My own chick flick

forward to this holiday. I think I'm going to love these American holidays. Miss McCarty tells us that Thanksgiving is more important for the American people than Christmas. It is for me too this year! I need to know more so I Google it. I read about its origins. And in class, *la professeur* has a great idea to simplify the concept. She has us perform a play on the history of Thanksgiving in front of all the other foreign students. I am an American Indian. I hold corn in my hands. Yuriko has never laughed so much in her entire life.

Anyway, I get the general idea, so now I wait to say thank you to Jeff for coming to see me over the holiday.

*

Today is my day! Jeff should be driving to me now. I check on the Internet, it takes 8 hours to drive from Philadelphia to Boston. When I think that my cute American boyfriend is driving 8 hours just to take me to dinner, I am flattered. Who wouldn't be? He must be in love with me. After spending 2 hours in the bathroom, I'm ready. I'm waiting outside at the university's front gate. A car comes, it's Jeff:

'*Bonjour* 'o wa leee," he says, smiling. 'Hope you haven't been waiting in the snow too long?'

'*Bonsoir* Jeff! Hope you had a good drive?' It's the least I can ask.

I warm up in the car. A pickup truck. Like Clark Kent in *Smallville*! So American. Love it! We don't have these in France. The roads are too small I guess. I wonder what the back part of the truck is for? Does Jeff haul firewood?

I didn't put too much makeup on, but I didn't have to. Just being next to him, my cheeks are pinkish red. He is so handsome—my American boyfriend in his big car. I'm feeling pretty cute in my little black dress. Of course, I don't know how I am going to be able to eat. It's only 6 p.m.

'You look beautiful. Just looking at you makes the long drive worth it.' He says.

Sweet, isn't he? I melt. He smiles.

We drive to Quincy Market. It's really crowded. I'm thinking it's going to be hard to find a spot to park when suddenly he stops the car in the middle of the street. I'm looking for the English word to express my surprise when a guy opens my door. I'm scared. I don't move. Jeff gets out of the car, walks to my side of the car, and gives his keys to the man. What is going on? Jeff smiles at me.

'Are you coming?' I get out of the car, and the man drives away in Jeff's car. Here we are, in front of a classy Italian restaurant.

'I booked this restaurant because the valet parking is convenient. And, of course, I thought you'd like to eat at a European restaurant!'

'Sure!' I say. Ohhhh . . . apparently that man wasn't stealing Jeff's car. 'I've never heard of valet parking. American guys know how to take a girl out.'

Inside, there are paintings all over, showing what looks like the American vision of the Italian coast. Candles on the table. The waiter says something. Jeff answers. I only understand the last sentence: 'She'll have the same.' Ok, he ordered for me. The waiter brings champagne and lobster ravioli. Good choice. He is so *chic*, my American boyfriend, wearing an Abercrombie & Fitch shirt. He tells me about Thanksgiving with his family. I pretend to understand. He laughs when he realizes that I have no clue what we are talking about. He asks: 'Blah blah blah such a beautiful French girl blah blah lost in Philadelphia?' I tell him that I am from Paris—it's much more exotic than Normandy. I explain why I came to the U. S. As a journalist, I need to speak fluent English. I make up some details to impress him. It works *bien sûr!* Of course! At the end of our meal, he asks: 'would you like me to show you the MIT campus? We could go up to the rooftop, the view is gorgeous!'

A romantic stroll on the rooftop of an MIT building? That sounds like more than '*une invitation*!' 'Yes, wonderful idea!' I say.

Students are still working in the classrooms. It's 10 p.m. Spending Saturday evening with a mathematical equation, no thank you. Those scare me. Lucky for me, I am in the arms of my American boyfriend. From the top of the building, we can see the Charles

River and the reflections of the city's lights color the sky. Everything is perfect! We stay here for hours, kissing. I am already so impatient to tell my *poulettes* about what I did with my *beau* American boyfriend on a rooftop of the MIT campus at night, in minus 10 degrees Celsius weather.

At 2 a.m., we arrive back at my campus.

'*Merci* Jeff! I spent a wonderful evening.'

'I had a great night too.'

We kiss for a long time, and I ask: 'We could meet again tomorrow before you take off?'

'Tomorrow?!'

Silence. I think he doesn't understand what I'm trying to convey. I was trying to put the right words together in my mind when he says:

'Tomorrow I'd like to leave early. I have an 8 hour drive ahead of me.'

'I understand. But when are we seeing each other again?'

'Well…' he says. So I describe my upcoming schedule: 'I go back to France for the Christmas holidays. I leave 2 weeks. But next weekend we could meet in New York?'

I think my idea is so romantic: meeting between Boston and Philadelphia.

'I guess I could do that.' He says.

We kiss goodbye. *Un baiser inoubliable!* An unforgettable kiss!

*

Back in my room Yuriko isn't sleeping. We debrief. 'Awesome,' I say, giving her all the details. Jeff and I are so good together. Conclusion: I'm in Love.

I am more motivated than ever in class. Miss McCarty says my English skills are improving. I would hope so! I go back to my main activity of 'writing long e-mails to Jeff'. His answers are shorter. And after a week, he doesn't answer at all. What is going on? What happened to him? I hope he hasn't been in an accident, and that nothing bad has happened to him or his family? He doesn't answer my phone calls. We haven't been in the habit of calling each other because I don't understand a word by phone, but the silence terrifies me. I keep writing to him:

From: Aurélie
To: Jeff
Subject: This Saturday
> *Bonjour Jeff,*
> *As we said, I'll wait for you under the Christmas tree at the Rocke-feller Center in New York.*
> *I can't wait to see you again,*
> *Aurélie*

Isn't this *rendez-vous* so romantic? *Oui!* I think so too. I'm a French girlfriend! Surely he is impressed by my romantic attitude. I am the opposite of an aggressive American girlfriend!

The Saturday morning of our *rendez-vous* I still haven't heard from him. I am a little disappointed, but I see what's going on here. He is testing me. He is planning to surprise me with a huge flower bouquet on his knees under the most beautiful Christmas tree in the world. Or something like that!

I buy a ticket to New York at the Chinese bus station. I was surprised when *la professeur* told me the easiest way to reach New York was to take a "Chinese bus." At first I didn't understand, but she explained that in the U.S., buses are a good and inexpensive way to travel from city to city. And the cheapest bus is from Chinatown, Boston to Chinatown, New York. I want to live like an American, so here I am, 4 hours later, in Chinatown, New York. It doesn't look anything like I had pictured New York would look. But, a few blocks later... *Oh mon Dieu!* I see what I was expecting, but even taller! I walk with my head up, looking at the sky where the buildings disappear. My first time in New York! Let's focus. I'm here for my American boyfriend. I reach to Fifth Avenue. Then I see it. I stand, open-mouthed, in awe of the tree. I wonder what the English word is for "bigger than big." In French, it's *gigantesque*. The Christmas spirit is everywhere!

1:47 pm. I'm early. A compact crowd arrives and walks to admire the tree. I see colorful hats dancing over a huge ice rink. 2:04 p.m. Where is he? I circle the tree. 2:21 p.m. No one. Don't panic, I think, he's just late. It's hard to find parking in New York, so I'm sure he is struggling to join me. 2:43 p.m. *Non!* I call. He doesn't pick up. He can't just not show up? 3 p.m. I hold on to my belief that he's coming. 3:57 p.m. He's not coming. Why would he do this? I don't understand. What about our kisses? What about my American boyfriend!?

French Girl Rendez-vous

From: LapetiteAurélieUSA
To: *"Poulettes"*
Subject: Sad Christmas Holiday

Giiiiirls,

I'm coming back for 2 weeks! I hope we'll be able to get together between champagne and *bûche de Noël**! I neeeeed you.
We have an American boyfriend *emergency* here! Something went wrong with Jeff.
He left me, standing alone under the Christmas tree in New York…
After the wonderful evening we spent in Boston 2 weeks ago, we were supposed to meet in New York before I leave…He never come…I'm coming back home in 3 days and I can't reach him…
I am heartbroken…*J'ai le coeur brisé…*
I don't understand where it went wrong…Why didn't he come? It doesn't make sense…
Could I have said something wrong without realizing? A translation error? It's true that sometimes I try new English words and I'm not sure they're right…I'm still learning… But come on! I couldn't have said something sooo bad that would warrant him running away…

Prepare the chocolates and *la crème brulée…*
American guys suck…

FYI: I gained weight. 6 pounds. I have no clue how many kilos it is. No comment please…

Still, come with chocolates… I need those.
I will call as soon as I arrive in Paris.
Aurélie, *très triste*

*The traditional French Christmas cake, a yule log

6. *Bonne année – ou pas...*[1]

My Christmas vacation with my family and friends in France was refreshing. Now I'm ready to learn more about these mysterious American guys. Aurélie in the U.S., round 2! No news from Jeff, obviously. Despite all the effort my *poulettes* made to get him out of my head, I'm still pondering why he didn't show up for our Christmas *rendez-vous* in New York.

Yuriko doesn't look happy on her return from Japan either. She doesn't say anything, so I don't ask. It doesn't feel like the right time.

In class, Miss McCarty has a new challenge for us: read a book. In English. Every word. *The Notebook*, by Nicholas Sparks. I spend my evenings trying to decipher this wonderful book.

I don't understand the whole love story, so I can't enjoy the book as much as I could... I have to look up every third word in my Harraps dictionary...

We are supposed to read the first two chapters—*Miracles* and *Ghosts*, 35 pages—for next week. Clearly, I won't be doing any shopping this weekend.

On top of that, I apply for a new class, "Conversation with an American girl." Every Wednesday afternoon, an American girl leads a conversation class. There's no teacher. This is supposed to help up improve our accents. I'm worried that speaking English with Yuriko all the time has caused me to develop a French-Japanese accent, so here I am. It's just girls. We listen to Kate, our American moderator, who divides us into groups of four. We can talk about anything we want, and she meanders around to help us with our pronunciation. *Bien sûr*, the subject of our conversations very quickly turns to guys. We are all from different countries, but

1 Happy - or not - new year

49

we all share one characteristic—we don't understand guys! I realize, not without disappointment, that apparently no nationality has superior knowledge in this area. We all have something to complain about.

This makes me nervous… Where is this perfect man we all dream of? The one from the Hollywood movies?

At this moment, Kate makes her way to my group's side of the room. She is now my American reference. Surely she will reveal the key to American guys. We are all convinced that, here, in the U.S., we'll find the perfect guy we've been looking for. Kate extinguishes our hopes in one sentence:

"Oh, God, American guys are the worst!"

These are not the words we were expecting. It doesn't matter. I need to ask her what happened with Jeff. She is the only one who can tell me what went wrong. So, I tell her my story. The short version: we met during a two-day trip to Philadelphia. He drove eight hours to see me. We made out on the top of an MIT building. Then, silence. And, of course, our unsuccessful *rendez-vous* under the Christmas tree in New York. Me, heartbroken. Him, the cause.

"Oh, come on!" She exclaims. "You're a Parisian girl—you had two dates with this guy, and suddenly you think he's the man of your life? That's ridiculous!"

Pardon? Excuse me? Is she making fun of me? I get stuck on the word "*date.*"

"Excuse me, Kate," I say, "what does it mean, 'date?'"

I look around at the other girls, and it's clear that they don't understand either.

"What? I wasn't expecting to have to explain what a date is." She looks embarrassed, thinks for a minute, and then says:

"A *date* is … Let me think how to put this…when you date a guy, it means you go out with him, ok? You meet up with him, you make out, etcetera, you know?"

"Yes it means he is your boyfriend! This is same in my country!" says an Asian girl. Clearly, this came right from the heart. She blushes and covers her mouth with her hand. I think she's Korean… *Bref,* we turn our focus back to Kate, who explains: "No!

He's you're just *dating* him, right?"
I can tell by the looks on the other girls' faces that still, none of us understand the difference. I ask a few follow up questions:
"I don't see what is different between these two guys. The guy you go out with and you kiss is your boyfriend."
I am puzzled. Certainly there aren't 500 different definitions of the word 'boyfriend,' right?
"No, your *boyfriend* is a guy you've been dating for awhile, who you've decided to get serious with. Dating is less serious—'cause you can date as many guys as you want, you know?"
Silence.
"Excuse me?" we reply, in unison.
"Yeah, as long as you haven't had 'the talk' about being exclusive, then you're not! You're just *dating*." Kate explains.

Now I'm totally lost. Walking back to my room, I wonder if that was the issue with Jeff? "Just 2 dates?" Kate had asked. Does this mean he's just some guy who enjoys driving eight hours to take a girl to a nice restaurant?! And that's it? That's all it was? I've kissed guys who didn't take me anywhere, so where does that leave me? Is it possible that American guys are actually harder to understand than French guys?

*

Yuriko is asleep when I get home. This is not a good sign. I don't want to bother her, so I go to the library. The weeks pass quickly, and I remain in deep reflection. We continue reading *The Notebook*. I'm kind of proud of myself. Now, I'm only looking up every sixth word on average—big progress. The storyline is so sweet. *Une histoire d'amour!* (A love story) Two soul mates, together forever, to face the world. It makes me believe in love again. Yuriko needs to read this book too. Tonight, she's crying:
"Kenta, *sniff sniff*... He broke up with me... *sniff sniff*..."
I'm momentarily speechless, but push myself to say something:
"Honey, slow down... What happened?"

"He said he couldn't wait anymore! Lilly, what am I going to do?"
I can't believe it. Just two more months before school ends, and she goes back to Japan. And now he decides he can't wait any longer? What goes on inside a man's head? It's a mystery.
Desperate times call for desperate measures, as they say. I invite our Korean suitemates, Claudia and Sofia, to our room for a little sleepover. I bought *The Notebook* DVD, and we all bring "junk food." Every girl learned this slang term very quickly. We were all very happy to meet Ben and Jerry, the two best friends of a heart-broken American girl. Then we go to the liquor store. At first I found it kind of strange to have to go to a special store to buy alcohol. In France, we just buy it at the supermarket. But at least here they have "BYOB" restaurants—a decent tradeoff!
Bref, we have junk food and alcohol. Everything we need for a great sleepover.
Perfect! We finish the night by bawling our eyes out. What a beautiful movie. Sofia tells us that the two main actors actually fell in love during the shooting. We all believe it.
Before we go to bed, a great idea is born. It begins with Claudia saying "Could we do this for Valentines day?"
"I have a better idea!" says Yuriko "What about going to San Francisco over the Valentines day weekend?"
Done. It's booked. And we're counting the days before our departure to California!

From: LapetiteAurélieUSA
To: *"Poulettes"*
Subject: American and French boyfriends are not equivalent

Salut poulettes!

Problem: my American boyfriend has never been Jeff. We had a cultural misunderstanding. Have you ever heard of a 'date'?
It appears that here, there's an additional step before a guy becomes your boyfriend. There's a time where you just *date* him. Yes, you go out with him. But it is not serious. And you and he can date other people too.
Interesting, isn't it?
I am still in shock. Jeff and I, we just had two dates--that apparently means nothing...and we won't have a 3rd one.
I did a little survey; "it seems like Japanese guys, French guys, and American guys are all equally difficult to deal with. Where are we supposed to go?

Talk to you soon,
Bisous,
Aurélie

7. *Dans l'action!* [1]

This morning I received an e-mail from Stan, the communications manager of the association in Philadelphia. Has he read the article? Maybe he doesn't like it? Let's see:

From: Stan<Science USA Association>
To: Aurélie
Subject: Scholarship

> *Aurelie:*
> *Your editor in chief sent me a few copies of the magazine, including the article about our event.*
> *I practiced my French trying to read it. It looks great.*
> *I'd like to let you know that we are offering some travel grants and scholarships.*
> *You should apply.*
> *Check our website.*
> *Best regards,*
> *Stan*

I don't understand every word in the email at first pass. So I check with my new favorite website, wordreference.com. The mauve page pops up. Let's figure out what Stan said. A grant = *une bourse*. Is he suggesting that I apply for some kind of scholarship with his company? I bring up their website. 'Travel grants… offering six month scholarships…' It means that I could go and spend six months in Philadelphia? Why not? Between going there and heading back to France without an American boyfriend… It's not a tough choice.

On her side, Yuriko has decided not to go back home. She doesn't want to return to her previous life without Kenta. I know what she

---

1 On the move

means, and I support her. On top of that, she and I feel that our time here is not over. It's not the right time to go back home. There are a ton of options for her to stay in the country, and she counsels me on a few.

Maybe she should become a Japanese teacher? Or a cello teacher? She's been playing for fifteen years.

In the end, she decides to stay a student for six more months.

I think she speaks English very well. Well, we have been learning together and we converse in English all the time. So I understand her accent and she understands mine. I would love to stay a student here forever! I don't feel like I'm 100% bilingual. *La professeur* makes me laugh when she asks us if we dream in English... She says it's a sign. Well my sign is that I understand what the Americans say on the T, and sometimes I surprise myself, listening to conversations in the cafeteria.

Why not stay a little longer? Or at least try to? The more I talk about it with Yuriko, the more I want to stay too. I gather the documents they need and I apply for the scholarship. Six more months of opportunity to meet my American boyfriend, I can't refuse!

*

To celebrate the end of the semester, the University organized a huge party. *Bien sûr!* We are all really excited in the dorm. Just a few more weeks and we go back home. Well, most of us do. Yuriko is so happy to stay for another semester. And I feel more and more anxious waiting for Stan's answer to my application. Whatever happens, Yuriko and I will keep in touch. We have a pact, and even if life separates us, we will invite each other to our respective weddings! We just need to find the two lucky men.

*

I'm reading an online article, listing the most dangerous cities in the country based on how many people are shot annually. Number 1:

Philadelphia. Oh great! I'd rather go back to Normandy than die in Philadelphia.

Dring Dring My heart beats faster. Where is my cell phone? Oh, right in front of me. I stare at it. It's Stan. I take a deep breath and try to put on my best American accent—the key is to pretend like I have a hot potato in my mouth:

"Hi! Stan!"

Stan says words. Many words that form many sentences. Why it is so much harder to understand someone on the phone? Do people talk faster on the phone? Stan does speak quickly. There is only one word that interests me, and I do understand it:

"Yes," he says.

I got the scholarship!

*

Yuriko shares my happiness, but we both cry thinking about going our separate ways. But I'm not going to the other end of the earth. Direction: Philadelphia, PA!

I find an apartment not too far from work. I decide to live with a *colocataire*, a roommate, again. And it promises to be fun—this time, it's a guy! Maybe my American boyfriend—we're thrown together by destiny! Wouldn't that be the cutest 'how did you meet' story ever? I found him on Craiglist. Here, you can rent, buy, exchange, or even borrow anything through this website. A job, a sofa, an American boyfriend! Craiglist is the website of the Americans on the move!

It's a lot of fun to look for my new roommate, like looking for a guy on Match.com! I have Miss McCarty correct my first response to an ad before I send it. The reply email is cute. I succeeded in talking to him on the phone. It was a nice talk—he speaks slowly, and I am grateful. Thirty years old, living alone in a big apartment because his girlfriend left him. Now he would like to rent his spare room, and I imagine comforting him with a bottle of French wine... His accent is cute and understandable. Seduced, I agree to take the room.

Boston airport. Two hours later, Philadelphia airport.

I take a cab to my new apartment. No more handing little cards with destination addresses to cab drivers! Now I can say it myself. In six months, what a progress! Proudly, I say to the driver:

"Five hundred and sixty three Euclid Street. Please."

"Hi! *Tu es Française ? Bonjour* !"

"*Oui* !"

"Your accent, I recognize it. An American would have said "5th and Fitzwater," See?"

"Oh! Thank you, I didn't know…"

I am kind of sad not to have said the address properly… what a lonely moment… But I miss speaking French, so who cares if I didn't give an address exactly as an American would? I'm happy to speak French with him:

"*Tu parles francais aussi?*" – Do you speak French too?

"*Oui je viens du Sénégal! Ca fait plaisir de parler un peu! Ca fait 10 ans tu vois que je suis ici!*" – Yeah! I'm from Senegal. It's nice to speak a little French! I've been here for 10 years!

"*Cool! C'est impressionnant!*"

I am impressed. He has no accent when he speaks English. Maybe in 10 years I will speak like an American too? He gives me his card. He drops me in front of a gate. At the corner, some young guys are listening to music in a parking lot. Like in the movies! The address is correct. No doubt. I ring the doorbell. All the hope I've invested in this roommate is ruined when a weird-looking guy answers the door. He is no Joey from *Friends*…he has lifeless eyes that don't even seem to be looking in the same direction? Where is my cute American guy with the charming voice? This is not what I ordered. The ad said, "I am in my thirties." Doesn't this mean he's thirty? I don't understand. He asks me to follow him, and I have no choice. He is not my American boyfriend, I already know that. Some people have a voice that doesn't fit their physical appearance…

From: LapetiteAurélieUSA
To: "*Poulettes*"
Subject: I'm never lucky with first roommates ...

Mes amies,
I am so glad I could extend my stay in the U.S. and discover another American city.
Philadelphia is more the "America" I imagined—the streets are perpendicular and numbered. It's more typical than Boston!
I'm also told that the atmosphere is very different here... and it was here that I met Jeff...
I'm happy, you know, but I feel strange today...
I just arrived at my new place, and it just doesn't feel right. I told you I found a roommate on the Internet... I was hoping we would fall in love... well, no way!

I'm freaking out! This place is dirty – now I understand why the ex-girlfriend dumped him. And the guy is weird too.
I wasn't expected this...
Maybe tomorrow I'll feel differently . . .
Aurélie, in a parallel world

8. *Bienvenue dans la ville de l'amour fraternel* [1]

I can rest all weekend before starting my new internship! I take advantage of the opportunity to visit the city. My roommate, Pat, is weird. He looks weird; he smells weird. But he does seem to have a good heart. He told me he organized a party to welcome me. How nice? Maybe I'm being too judgmental. He would like to introduce me to his friends so I can meet people in the area.

The party is at 6 p.m. I decide to cook a French dish, something easy like a *Quiche Lorraine* and a *Quatre quart*. Cooking for his friends is the least I can do. It will add a French touch!

I exit to the sidewalk through our gate. I stop. Why is this street so crowded? Why is there so much activity in front of my place? I get closer to the crowd. The police are there. I get closer. An ambulance. What is going on? *Oh mon Dieu!* There's blood. All over the street. They've strung the same yellow barrier tape as I've seen in *Cold Case Files!* I want to vomit. I did hear a noise last night. I run back to the apartment.

Laying on the sofa, a glass of something unidentifiable in his hand, Pat is watching TV. It's 11 a.m. I tell him about the scene outside as I sit down in the chair next to the sofa.

"Yeah… it happens…" He says. "Hope the cops won't stick around too long… It might not be good for tonight's party."

I am speechless. As he speaks, I recognize a familiar smell. At this moment, there is a connection in my brain. I stand up, and Pat gets up from the couch. I stay still. He takes a bottle of whisky from the shelf and goes back to the couch. He nods, inviting me to sit down with him. I do. He takes an empty glass from the table and pours the liquor:

1 Welcome in the city of brotherly love

"You want a drink?" he says.

I stare at him, refusing the glass with a wave of my hand. He insists. He brings his face way too close to mine. I can't take it anymore. I need to find a way to leave. I smile and I stand up politely, but quickly. He barely reacts. Maybe he is so drunk that he can't even stand up again. I go to my room and pack. I escape with my two bags. I wonder if he can hear, if he has figured out that I am leaving? I have no idea, and he doesn't move a muscle as I leave with my luggage. I call the nice cab driver that dropped me off yesterday. I ask him in French to please pick me up as soon as he possibly can.

"A l'aéroport s'il vous plait!" – "Back to the airport, please!"

*

Is Pat dangerous? I don't think so. But I can't live in that mess, especially not with a drunk.

Back to square one. In tears. I call Yuriko. She is so good to me. She calms me down and makes me laugh! She searches for a place for me to stay tonight. I want to go home! "No!" she says. She finds a hotel on the Benjamin Franklin Parkway, one of the main streets of Philadelphia. She reads: "The Benjamin Franklin Parkway was built in honor of the *Champs-Elysées*. Flags from countries all over the world hang there…"

It's a sign. This street is inspired by Paris. She tells me to book two nights in this hotel, and ask my coworkers on Monday for advice on finding a place for six months. *Oui!* She is right. I am not going to give up my internship because of an alcoholic (*un boulet*)!

I spend the rest of the weekend in my hotel room, too afraid to leave in the off chance I might run into Pat.

This weekend, Yuriko met her new roommate, a Brazilian girl who took my place. *Bien sûr*, she immediately says that the new girl will be less fun than me and that she misses me so much.

From: LapetiteAurélieUSA
To: "*Poulettes*"
Subject: Address changing

Hi *mes poulettes!*
I had a hard time settling in this city, but now I am fine!
I just made a mistake in choosing my roommate…no American
boyfriend—just a *boulet*! So forget the address I gave you to forward my *Elle* magazine, I will send you a new one.
Now, I found the perfect place for me. My own place—a one-
bedroom apartment. Better to be alone than in bad company, right?
Jenny -a very nice girl from the office- helped me find it. She is
really nice to me, thirty, athletic, and fun. She took me under her
wing. She spent a semester in France when she was a student. She
remembers almost nothing of the French language but she knows
how it feels to be a foreigner, and she loves France!

Let's make a Skype appointment to visit my new home! I have one
big closet, and the view is great. It's right on the Parkway, a touristy
area of the city- not dangerous at all!
The best part: there is a doorman. Safety first!
XOXO (this is the latest signoff phrase of the American girls - X
means hugs and O means kisses! (Don't ask me why…))

Aurélie, ready for action

9. *Orgueil et préjugé* [1]

Just like every morning, Stan welcomes me with a smile. I love my little desk in the corridor where all the travel grant recipients are situated. Everyone is so friendly. Some remember meeting me at the conference last November. I remember meeting Jeff...

The job is great. I have to write articles on the image of chemistry for the internal magazine. In English - this is the tricky part. But *Oui!* I feel more and more confident in my writing. And I am so excited that I'm going to be published in English.

I'm the only French person among the 60 employees. Some people stop by to introduce themselves. Some are curious, and just stop by to have a look at 'the French girl'. *C'est marrant!* It's amusing! Some talk to me like I'm a child, outrageously articulating their words. Others act as if I'm not here.

As for the work, I gain a totally new perspective on the American way of life. In Boston, I was spending my time with foreigners who were also learning the language, and I'd not yet spent a lot of time with Americans! The only consistent thing is that they call me Lilly here too.

I slowly realize that most of the people I work with have no clue where France is. Well, I suppose I don't know where all of the American states are either. A coworker once forgot my name and referred to me as 'the European girl.' That's ok with me. When Jenny – the coworker who helped me find an apartment, who I am now friends with—talks about her stay in Paris, she always says 'When I was in Europe' and never 'When I was in France'!

Here, the news comes on at 6 p.m., the American dinner time. In France, the news comes on at 20h00 (8 p.m.). I watch a lot of

1 Pride and prejudice

television. It helps me to understand where I am. But every ten minutes, there's a commercial break! This is so strange to me. If a movie were on television in France, they would show the entire movie with only one commercial intermission. Here, you have ten breaks to go pee…?! At first I didn't get it. There isn't even an introduction before the commercials. In France, commercials are introduced by a little cartoon of the word 'PUB,' meaning 'Ads'. We call it *'un jingle.'* Isn't it an English word? But here, there is no introduction. The first movie I watched in the U.S. was set in colonial times. Suddenly, a man ran across the screen and jumped into a car. "Where the hell did that guy come from?!" I was wondering, but then I saw an advertising motto… Anyway… what I love is that I am so far ahead on all the great TV shows. Even on some that don't exist yet in France.

*

Things are crazy at work today. Stan is organizing a 3-day conference hosted by our office. Dozens of journalists from the best American magazines will attend the presentations. There will be a cocktail hour followed by a dinner each evening for three days.

First day. Chris, 35 years old, a coworker, stays close to me. Jenny keeps her eyes on me. I have a pretty clear idea what Chris is up to. I've been aware of his game since I arrived. But I didn't worry too much, because he has a wedding ring. So I assumed he came by my office out of curiosity. Now he comes to see me, carrying two flutes of champagne:
"Thank you, Chris," I say, taking the glass he offers me.
"How've you been doin' since you joined us? It's already been three weeks. You're doin' ok?"
He stands really close to me. There are a lot of people, and we're packed around the buffet.
"*Oui*! Yes, I mean. I enjoy living in Philadelphia—you have a great city." I say politely.
"Yeah! Hey, you wanna go grab dinner somewhere else? We can't

hear each other here! I'll take you to an awesome restaurant–it's not far from here."

"Excuse me? You know there's a dinner after this cocktail?"

"Sure but I thought we could spend some blah blah blah just the two of us." He smiles, showing his teeth. I think I recognize the words he said, but I'm not sure of the meaning. I think he said 'quality time', *temps de qualité?* I don't really understand the literal meaning, but I think I get the idea.

"Chris, I'm flattered. But I'm also a little shocked. I can see you're married!" I gesture towards his wedding ring.

"Oh come on! You're French. Married or not, you don't care, right?"

This American guy seems genuinely surprised by my inability to respond. I just walk away and recount the story to Jenny.

She laughs. I laugh. Two glasses of champagne later, she tells me all the work gossip.

I learn that Chris sleeps with an intern every summer. She tells me who is sleeping with whom, and who was sleeping with whom. We have a lot of fun at this cocktail hour. Jenny isn't phased by any of this gossip. She's in love with her longtime boyfriend, who she calls her "honey." We spend dinner talking about our colleagues. *Bref,* I have a good time.

Second day. Lots of people, lots of champagne. Guess who arrives with Chris? His wife! Isabella, a beautiful woman with long dark hair, looks to be of Mexican origin. He introduces her to me. I hate this guy. I run to tell Jenny, but she doesn't react as I expected:

"Isabella is here? Nice! I haven't seen her in a long time," she says.

"You know her?"

"Yeah, of course. You can bring your better half to any of the work events."

I am confused. I have to ask:

"Everyone knows he is unfaithful. Isn't he scared she might discover it at this event?"

"Why would she? No one is going to say anything. It's not their business."

Ok…what should I say? It's kind of sad. I mean, he's basically making fun of her by bringing her here—everyone knows but her. What a *boulet*! He's not even that good looking… If I were this woman, I would appreciate it if someone had the courage to come tell me. But Jenny says:

"Well, you never know. You're not in her shoes, you know? Just let it go, ok?"

I love this expression, "to be in someone's shoes." *Dans ses chaussures*. It always conjures an image of me physically wearing the other person's shoes. It makes me laugh every time I hear it!

Anyway, I decide not to tell Isabella that her husband is a jerk, but I have less fun for the rest of the evening.

Third day. Cocktail. . . Forget it, I'm not going.

*

A call from Yuriko cheers me up for the weekend. Life is great at the University. She isn't getting along with her roommate though… But she doesn't really care. She doesn't spend much time in her room anymore. She has a boyfriend! *Bonne nouvelle!* Great news! And a French one! A guy named Henri seduced my Yuriko. I want to tell her not to be that excited, because French guys are evil. All of them are *boulets*… I want to tell her: "get out of there fast!" But then I think of Jenny and her "other people's shoes" warning, so I keep my tone neutral:

 "Enjoy! Have fun! I am happy for you…"

Well, I can't say that I've found a better nationality at the moment. I remain baffled.

From: LapetiteAurélieUSA
To: *"Poulettes"*
Subject: I don't recognize myself… Help!

Mes petites poulettes,

To be honest, my search for an American boyfriend appears to be more difficult than expected.
A l'aide! Help! I am now a member of The Philadelphia Art Museum, so I go every weekend to stare at a Monet painting from Normandy…
What's wrong with me?
Did you know that Philadelphia is the "birthplace of American history"? I visited the Liberty Bell, the symbol of United States Independence. It's a cracked bell…

And I went to Independence Hall. I took a picture of the inkpot in which the men representing the thirteen first states dipped their pens and signed The Declaration of Independence. I will send you the picture.

Aurélie, in need of a man

10. *Jouer à l'Américaine* [1]

I feel very well. I enjoy the rhythm of life people have in the U.S. And I love the job. Nowadays I am writing articles for an Australian and a Canadian magazine. It's a nice assignment! Stan is happy with the international perspective I provide to the company. I'm glad Stan's happy. On the work level, being here offers me a great opportunity that I would not have in France. I try to remember how lucky I am, but what I want is an American boyfriend. And I have only two months left to find him. So now it's my only focus. I put myself out there. I am "in" for every happy hour. From 5 p.m. to 7 p.m., I discover that Americans enjoy "doing happy hour" with their colleagues. In August, it's *40 ℃* (104°F!) here, and a cold drink is mandatory at the end of the day. So, *oui! J'aime les happy hours!*

"What would you like?" asks Jenny, as we sit at a bar across from the office.
Jenny and I get along well with the other scholars, and it's a good atmosphere. They are all from different states, so I like talking to them about where they come from. And tonight I am in a real party mood!
"A Lager, please!" I answer proudly.
A Lager is a beer from Pennsylvania. It's actually called a *Yuengling Lager*, but Philadelphians just say "Lager," and the waiter knows what they want. I love knowing these kinds of details, it makes me feel like a real American girl.
"There's a concert on Penn's Landing! Feel like going?" says Jenny.
A concert? *Bien sûr!*

1 An American game

There is a big crowd at the waterfront, some music, a stage, many young people, many young guys, and way too many Lagers. A great night!

"Hi! I'm Tom. Blah blah blah music?" asks a tall guy behind me.

"Hi! I'm Lilly." I say with the hot potato accent. I definitely feel that all the Lagers make me speak better English.

"Do you blah blah blah?"

Jenny gives me a positive-looking wink, so I guess at an answer:

"I enjoy this kind of concert. I don't know the group, but they are kinda good!"

I feel like I'm speaking like a real American girl by pronouncing 'kind of' as 'kinda,' having noticed that Americans do that a lot.

"Nice accent. Where are you from?" He says.

He ruins my self-esteem in one sentence. I drink more, and resist to my desire to break his neck:

"I come from France," I say.

"Oh nice! That's cool!" he says. "What are you blah blah?"

Maybe I had too many Lagers. I don't understand. He gives it another shot:

"What are you doing in Philadelphia? Vacation?"

"No, work!"

"Me too! I'm from Davenport, Iowa!"

"Ok! Where is it?"

"It's in the Midwest. The city I was born in is on the border with Illinois."

"Sorry I have no idea where Illinois is either…" I say, feeling 'kinda' stupid.

"Have you heard of Chicago?"

"*Oui*! Yes! I know Chicago!"

Not paying attention, we find ourselves separated from the crowd.

We sit on a bench overlooking the river. He looks great, this American guy, "Tom." He has beautiful, huge green eyes, and he smiles a lot.

"Can I get your number? I know some great places—I could show you around!" He says.

He doesn't need to justify anything! I give him my number with pleasure.

*

The following morning at 9 a.m., Jenny comes into my office with two coffees and two muffins.

"I want to hear all the details!" she says as a hello.

"Tom is so adorable." My cheeks redden.

"And?"

"He asked for my number, but he hasn't called yet…"

"He'll call!"

Jenny is certain that Tom will call. I hope so too! But when? I put my cell phone in the position on my desk where it gets the best service. *Midi*, noon, still no news. Jenny says: "Don't worry. He'll call." Doubt engulfs me. I should have gotten his number too. Maybe he expected me to ask for his number in return. I didn't, so now he thinks that I don't want him to call. I am so stupid. Why didn't I ask for his number? Such a stupid, amateur mistake…

I call Jenny from our internal work line:

"I have a vital question on cultural differences…"

"Let's get coffee!"

Coffee break at Starbucks, *bien sûr*!

"When will he call back?" I ask.

"Three day rule, Lilly!" Jenny answers, quick as a flash, adding skim milk to her coffee. She explains:

"If the guy calls you one or two days later, it means he's needy. After three days, it means he has a life, which is what you want. You don't want him to be a loser!"

Ok! Waiting for his call is making me crazy. I can't write. I turn my cell phone volume up and down every hour, just to make sure it's working.

Jenny tells me she and her "honey" met at a New Year's Eve party. It took a week before he called back. It's funny that Jenny only refers to him as her "honey." I have never heard his real name, if he has one. I never asked. The French translation is *'Miel.'* It's surprising from a French point of view to call your boyfriend *Miel*!

It makes me laugh… single me… I wish Tom were my *Miel*… Ok, my scholarship ends in few weeks… I return to France soon… and then? If we love each other, if he is the man of my life, he'll come with me! Or I would stay here with him! He will marry me! Such a wonderful love story has no borders.

I go home directly after work today. I learn about Iowa on Google. Wikipedia tells me that the capital has a French name, Des Moines, isn't it a sign? It's been two days since we met. I want to shout: "Caaaaaallllll me!" I feel ready though, I know the rules now. I have - I could say - dating experience. I have all the cards and now I can play! I am ready to date an American guy so that he'll become my American boyfriend.

Dring Dring ! Actually no, my cell phone ring is "*All the single ladies,*" by Beyonce. *Bref,* my cell rings.

"*Allo?*" Oops, this is a bad reflex. I correct myself immediately: "Hi?"

"Hey Lilly, it's Tom. We met at the concert, do you remember me?"

"Tom! Yes, of course. How are you?"

I have only one goal for this conversation—to keep it going until I get a *rendez-vous*. I surprise myself! I never even stress this much for a job interview! I take a big breath.

"I have two tickets for the game this weekend. Would you like to go?" He says.

Un jeu? A game? What game? Monopoly?

"Excuse me, I don't understand! A game?" I say.

"I have two tickets for the baseball game this Sunday. Do you wanna come with me?"

"Baseball?"

"Have you ever been to a baseball game?"

"No…"

"Oh, Lilly you have to go!"

"I don't know anything about baseball…"

"It's going to be fun. Let's meet for brunch before. I'll explain the rules and then we'll go, ok?"

"Ok!"

 "Sunday at Sabrina's? 11 a.m.?"

"Where?"

"Sabrina's Café. I'll text you the address, ok?"

"Ok!"

"See you then!"

My neurons are burning from the intense concentration I put forth to understand the phone call. I need a nap... But I did it! I have a date! A real one!

From: LapetiteAurélieUSA
To: "*Poulettes*"
Subject: The ball is in my court!

My Honeys (affectionate American nickname)
I'm back in business! His name is Tom. I met him at a concert. We have a date this Sunday for brunch. Then he'll take me to a baseball game. I have three days to learn the rules.
Does this sport even exist in our country?

Anyway, I went to *le coiffeur* to get my hair done! New haircut, new luck in love!
The salon here is weird. First, you tip everyone. The person who says hello, the one who shows you where to sit, the one who washes your hair, and then the one who cuts your hair. Here, you tip (*un pourboire*) everywhere—it's not included like at home.
So the weird thing is, the guy cut my hair dry. Not wet. Dry!
He says it's a technique from Paris! I told him that I'm from Paris and had never had my hair cut like this! He turned a little red, and the women in the salon shot him a weird look.
What do you think? $ 85… Was it worth it?

Cross your fingers for me on Sunday!

Aurélie

11. *Un classique Américain* [1]

I try to find out more about this sport that Americans love so much—baseball. As a good journalist, I investigate. The Philadelphia baseball team is called *the Phillies*. Ok. I can remember that. Their color is red. (This is important to know so I don't wear the "wrong" color for the game.) Their mascot is a strangely amoebic and androgynous green animal called *the Philly Phanatic*. But, most importantly, I learn that Philadelphian girls' favorite player is Chase Utley. Ok. But what are the rules? That's more difficult to understand. I read on the internet: "two teams of nine players...four bases...the pitcher...the batter...and there is a something about a *run*... 'homerun'...and an 'out'..." I pull up a strange diagram on my computer screen, and quickly abandon my efforts to understand it. I convince myself that I know enough for a first date.

Sunday morning I put on a red t-shirt so I'll fit in at the game. Tom is lovely, and we have a good time at brunch—we really "clicked." A friend told me that it is scientifically proven that if you can keep eye contact with someone more than 8.1 seconds, you are more likely to fall in love. I believe it. I do my best to maintain eye contact with him, but I can't do it for more than 6 seconds...

The subway is packed with people dressed like baseball players. It's a sea of red. Almost everyone is wearing some type of Phillies paraphernalia—the most popular being a Phillies baseball cap. I guess American guys feel naked without hats? Some kids are wearing a giant, fake, red foam hand. It's like a runway show of Phillies products! Tom wears a cap, *bien sûr*, and an "official" Phillies T-shirt.

When we arrive I am shocked to see so many people, and particularly shocked to see that there are just as many women as

1 An American classic movie

men—and way too many kids! I thought the stadium would be an exclusively male sanctuary.

"Want a soda and a hot dog?" Tom asks.

What? We each just had a three-egg omelet (according to the menu) at brunch, with potatoes and pancakes drowned in maple syrup.

"Good idea…thank you." I say.

Tom returns with a surprise for me: a Phillies cap! I wear it very proudly—like an American girl. Tom tries to explain the rules to me. I don't really understand, and finally I confess that I am not really paying attention. He laughs, and that's all that matters to me. I'm so happy to be with an American guy who is happy to explain his culture to me. My dream is coming true. I learn something interesting about baseball that my online research did not reveal: a game takes three hours. But time goes fast in good company, so it's fine. *Et le champion est,* and the winner is: The Phillies! Euphoria in the stadium! Euphoria in my heart! I can't explain why, but suddenly I find myself hugging Tom and spontaneously kissing him. He is definitely surprised, but I can't tell if it's a good surprise or the kind of surprise in which you feel really embarrassed to have been kissed for the first time in a very public place. Well, at least they won the game, and he invites me for another date next weekend. Something more intimate—dinner on Saturday night.

*

Jenny is so happy for me, and I'm happy for me too. After work, she joins me for some shopping at Anthropologie. We need to find the dress that will make me the perfect French girlfriend. This *boutique* is what I would call a *"petit bijou"*—a "piece of jewelry." It's four floors of happiness. As a French girl who used to live in Paris, Jenny considers me a shopping expert.

"Come on, you know what to wear," she says, eyes full of respect. I am amused that I can get her to buy virtually anything. All I have to say is, "this is very fashionable in Paris," and she buys it! Jenny is very attractive, and she has been nicer to me than any American thus far, so I would never do that. But it's nice to be treated like an expert! We head East on Chestnut Street for our second mission of the day: a French mani/pedi. There's a nail salon on every corner here—they are almost as prevalent as Starbucks' coffee. No need to make an appointment—you just walk in and an Asian girl immediately takes care of you. Here, it appears that manicure/pedicure-seeking is the female equivalent to discussing baseball. American women always appear to have perfectly polished nails—whether they're wearing a suit or jeans. I have nothing but respect for this. "*Respect.*" Jenny and I are sitting comfortably in giant massage chairs, relaxing our feet in hot water, when an idea pops into Jenny's mind:

"I already told you about the third-date rule, right?"

"I remember the 3 day rule…"

"No, no. See, now you're dating him—now you're at a totally different stage."

American woman really surprise me with all their rules.

"Ok, this is important—pay attention. You know the baseball rules, right?"

"*Oui*! I went to a game. I am a Phillies 'phan' now!"

"Yeah…ok the 3 basic rules of dating are similar to a baseball game! First date, first base: he gets your number."

"*Oui*! I say enthusiastically, I did this one!"

"Second date, second base: you kiss."

"*Oui*! I did this one!"

"And third base, third date, you sleep together!"

I am listening to Jenny as I admire the nail art created by the Asian girl at my feet. Suddenly the translation of what Jenny just said arrives in my brain:

"*Oh mon Dieu!* Third base is tonight!"

In front of the mirror, back at my place, we get organized. I bought a perfect little red Anthropologie dress—I stuck to red for luck. *La French manucure*: dry! I'm ready for date number three.

"Oh Lilly, you look perfect! You're gonna have a blast tonight!' says Jenny, proudly admiring my third date look.

Dix-huit heures. 6 p.m. I'm at the corner of 18th and Locust. The restaurant is called *Le Parc*—French. Excellent! It's perfect copy of a Parisian brasserie. I'm amazed—the terrace opens onto Rittenhouse Square, one of the quaintest parks in Philly.

"Lilly, you look fantastic!" Tom says with a smile.

'Fantastic!' Me? This old thing?…

"Bonsoir!" I say in French—very appropriate in this décor. I smell the romantic flavor of Paris all around us. Everything is from Paris—the music, the atmosphere, the paintings and our conversation:

"I'd love to visit your country," Tom says.

 "Well, I'll be back in France in a month. You could come—it will be September, it's a nice time for getting lost in Paris," I reply.

"Hmmm…I'll definitely consider your offer." He says, smiling.

We are making plans for the future, no? I'm not dreaming, right? We're talking about being together even when I return to France. *Je suis amoureuse!* I'm in love!

We talk all evening. We walk hand in hand, kissing, enveloped by the sweetness of the summer night's air. Finally, we arrive at his place. We continue kissing on the sofa. His apartment is huge, and I picture myself moving in. He puts on some music and offers me a Lager. We kiss and talk about everything we'll do in Paris when he visits me. We are still kissing when we stand as one and move slowly to another room—his bedroom, *bien sûr!*

We move in the shadowy light. *Oups!* Crash bam boom! My heel gets stuck in something on the floor, and we fall down together onto the parquet floor. In a common laugh, I reach my hand to my shoe to remove whatever made me fall. My hand grabs an object as Tom busies himself undressing me. It's weird—it feels like another shoe, a high-heeled shoe. I push Tom away to see what I'm holding in my hand.

Tom is surprised: "What's wrong, baby?"

I have in my hand a strappy, high-heeled sandal that is not mine…I stare at Tom, shocked and confused:

"What is this? Whose shoe is this?!"

Tom doesn't understand what the big deal is. He has a look at the shoe and says: "Oh, it's probably Pam's—no big deal, baby."

Did he forget to mention a teenaged sister?

"Who is Pam?" I ask.

"My girlfriend—I mean, we see other people, it's ok." He resumes our session.

I only remember the word 'girlfriend.'

"Excuse me, Tom," I say, pushing him away again, "you have a girlfriend?"

"Yeah…She's more a 'friend with benefits,' a roomie with benefits, you know!"

My brain can't translate this sentence.

He ends my confused silence, saying, "We're like a French couple, you know?"

Where do American people get the idea that French couples are free to date other people?

"Tom, you really think your girlfriend is ok with this? That we can have sex in her bed and that she is fine with it?" I yell at him. My curiosity is stronger than the ridiculous of the situation.

He understands that I am not so much in the mood now, so he stands up, trying to justify his statement, "She is! I swear! Our theory in life is that we are all Munchkins. We are all here to have a good time and enjoy life, right?"

Non non non, this is not right at all. I don't know what a Munchkin is, but I'm not enjoying my time on the floor with another girl's man (and shoe). I can't stay. Only French swear words come to my mouth as I leave.

*

Back in my apartment in my pajamas, I turn on my laptop. It's 10:30 p.m. I call Jenny. She is as shocked as I am, despite her American nationality. This comforts me a little. It means the problem is likely isolated to *this* American guy.

'I am so sorry to bother you so late, Jenny. But he said something that I really need to understand…"

"No problem, Lilly. I'm really sorry it didn't work out. What did he say?"

"He said that we are all 'Munchkins' and just here to have fun??"

"What? 'Munchkins?' Are you sure? That's really weird."

"Yeah I guess…what does it mean?"

"The only thing I can think that he was talking about is the little people from *The Wizard of Oz*."

"The Wizard of what? What are you talking about?"

"Oz. Ohh-Zee. Oz. Every American kid has seen this movie! It's a classic. Judy Garland plays the main character, Dorothy—a girl from Kansas who gets swept into another world by a tornado, and her only way home is by using these ruby-encrusted red slippers. Everybody here knows it."

Everybody but me… I Google the title as Jenny explains. I see "The Wizard of Oz, 1939." There is a picture of 4 characters, 3 men—dressed as a lion, a scarecrow, and some kind of robot—and a little girl with a blue dress and sparkling red shoes.

"Jenny I have never seen this movie!"

"Oh! You *sooo* have to download it or get the DVD!" she exclaims, enthusiastically.

"Ok, so what is the point with the Munchkins?"

"At one point, Dorothy meets these funny little men who live in, and sing about, 'Munchkin Land.' They basically just sing and dance all day."

"I see…Thank you for explaining…" I say, dejected and disheartened.

I hang up. I saw in Tom my American boyfriend, and he saw in me a Munchkin? I crawl into bed and wrap myself in a blanket.

From: LapetiteAurélieUSA
To: "*Poulettes*"
Subject: I want to come back home!

Mes poulettes,

Game over. I succeeded in speaking their language, but it hasn't helped me to understand them, the American guys. Tom is a cultural misunderstanding on top of the others... I really scored with these ones!
Let's face it: I will never find my American boyfriend. I go back to France for good in 3 weeks. A miracle won't happen...

It's fine you know...'cause I am looking forward to seeing you again!
It has been already a year! And what a year! My love life has been a disaster...

I am happy to move back but at the same time I feel I would enjoy staying here longer even without an American boyfriend! I love life here otherwise...

Anyway...please don't make plans for my 25th birthday!

Aurélie, single forever

12. *Désorientée* [1]

I find it hard to wake up in the morning. It's only two weeks before I return to France. My year in the U.S. went fast. I'm frustrated not to have had enough time to meet my American boyfriend. What happened? I think of all the things I didn't have the time to do. I didn't even visit the Guggenheim Museum in New York. It's too soon...I need more time. I am convinced *l'homme de ma vie*, the man of my life, is waiting for me here. I just didn't have enough time to meet him yet...

Monday morning at the office, Jenny brings me a coffee and a scone:

"Hey Munchkin," she says, jokingly.

"Right, make fun of me! How could he have a girlfriend?" I reply, sadly.

"I know, I'm so sorry. He's a jerk," she replies.

"Nothing happened the way it should have..."

I'm weepy, so Jenny doesn't risk upsetting me any more. She wisely invites me to lunch, and I accept.

I breathe deeply and put on my headphones for some calming music. The popular Natasha Bedingfield song—the one where she lets the world know she is single and happy about it—comes on. My love life is a mess on two continents. But *non*, I wouldn't trade my time in the U.S. for a different outcome. Still totally worth it.

*

Now I'm in bed but still working. My scholarship ends next week, so next Monday I have to give a one-hour presentation to all my coworkers on what I accomplished over the past six months. But my work can wait until tomorrow, because Monday is *Gossip Girl*

1 Lost in translation

85

time on CW, my favorite TV station in the U.S. I clearly have my priorities straight.

Even after my favorite show, I can't fall asleep. I realize that I'm feeling kind of afraid to go back home. I'm turning twenty-five very soon, and I didn't find an American boyfriend.

I can already hear the comments: "Aurélie is back in town! Remember how she left promising to return with an American guy? Well, where is he, her prince charming? She came back alone."

It's terrible! During this past year, two of my best friends met their perfect other halves. One of them is going to move in with the guy, and I haven't even met him yet. It feels weird, because I have met every *boulet* she has dated since the age of fifteen.

Also, I used to make fun of people who would say, 'Oh! I can't watch an American movie if it's not in original version. The dubbing is always off.' Well, now that I understand English, I love the voice of Jennifer Aniston in *Friends*, and it will be so strange to hear a French woman as Rachel...

And *bien sûr*, I gained 20 pounds. It's the bonus almost every girl in a new country gets. It's like a goodbye present to thank you for your commitment to learning the U.S. culture.

My return to Normandy will be tough I think...

My last week is here... I buy the biggest suitcase I can find. Perhaps I did too much shopping. And I sell or give away the few things I bought for my apartment... Yuriko impresses me: she stays! She decided she wants to become a photographer and got into a university in New York City. She is staying in the U.S., taking on a new career, and on top of that, her French boyfriend Henri is staying with her in Boston, which makes her happier than ever.

Meanwhile, I'm packing to go back to Normandy, France, the land of the cows...

*

Applause! All my coworkers are here to congratulate me at my scholarship presentation. Stan is very excited for me. I don't understand why—I'm sad because I only have five more days in the U.S. But, the easiest thing for me to do here when I don't understand someone's actions is to ignore them and assume it's a cultural difference. So, I go to the stage and begin:

"Testing 1, 2…"

I tap the microphone to check the sound quality and to get everyone's attention. Every employee of the Science History Association is here. Not that they are all interested in what I have to say, but Jenny organized a company happy hour with free food and drink around my presentation, so everyone is here, *bien sûr*! I can see all my coworkers plus one. I notice a "used to be very handsome" man with white hair, sitting next to Stan.

"I'd like to thank you all for everything you did for me. I spent six wonderful months working with you. I have learned so much. *Merci, au revoir*!"

I am on the verge of tears. I'm going to miss them, my American public!

Jenny and Stan present me with a baseball cap and a mug with 'Philadelphia' written on them—how could I leave without those? After few Lagers, Jenny tells me she has never enjoyed going to work so much as she has over the past six months with me. *Trop adorable*, we'll keep in touch, *bien sûr*.

I am drowning my sadness and mourning the loss of my non-existent American boyfriend in the mini-burgers at the buffet. At the bar, I order another Lager, but I can't remember if it's my fourth or fifth. Stan asks me to come with him.

"Lilly, I'd like to introduce you Bob, the director of the Communications department of PAJ Industries here in Philadelphia."

"Bonjour Bob!" I can't restrain a laugh. In my defense, '*un bob*' in French is a summer hat that old guys wear in the South while drinking *Pastis*, an anise-flavored alcohol, and staring out at the sea. No boss in France would be ever be called 'Bob.' So for me, this introduction is pretty amusing. And yeah… maybe I also had a bit too much Lager. Bob isn't offended:

"I liked your presentation. You speak English very well, and Stan is full of praise for you!" he says.

He is very friendly, and I imagine that in French he would address me with the more familiar "*tu*" instead of the formal "*vous*." How convenient it is that in English people address everyone as "you," regardless of their level of familiarity. I am debating the *tu/vous* distinction in my head when I realize that his is trying to make conversation.

"Thank you. Stan has been the perfect boss for me."

"You're going back to France this weekend, right?"

"Yes I am. You know I've been in the U.S. for a year now…"

"And you prefer to go back home?"

"*Non*! No, I mean, I am happy to go back to my country but I'd enjoy staying too…"

"Really?"

"Yeah! Your country is so huge! I haven't had enough time to visit all the cities I wanted to! This year went so fast!"

"Where would you like to go?"

"I wish I could go to Las Vegas and see the Grand Canyon!"

Bob laughs and Stan stares at me with big eyes. I don't bother and say:

"Where are you from, Bob? I hear an accent in you, too!"

"That's correct! You're good! I'm from Texas."

"Texas! They don't like French people in Texas!" I reply, not thinking.

I regret saying something that stupid, but a sip later I forget it.

"That's not true. I'm from Texas and I don't hate the French— I work for a French company."

"Which company?" I ask.

I forgot that Stan had already told me during the introduction.

"I work for P.A.J. Industries—don't you know it? It's a huge French company."

My bad, everyone knows this company.

"Sure! So do you speak French?" I ask.

"Unfortunately, I don't."

"You don't? I think it would be very helpful for you to have someone who speaks fluent French in your team," I suggested.

"Yes. A bilingual person would be a real advantage for us. I'm considering the possibility."

At this moment, Jenny grabs my hand, saying "excuse me" to Bob.

She pulls me aside and suggests we head for the salsa club we love. I am instantly seduced in my inebriated state. I don't even say goodbye to Bob and Stan, and happily leave to spend the rest of the night dancing with Jenny. We want to enjoy what time we have left as much as we can.

*

Next morning, first thing: headache pills. As I walk to the office, I replay the conversation I had with Bob. *Oh, mon dieu!* Is it possible that it was some kind of interview? I was so drunk, non! Did I just miss an opportunity to stay longer in the U.S.? I totally screwed up. I march directly to Stan's office. He welcomes me ironically:
"You made quite an impression yesterday…"
Oh no, that doesn't sound good…
"Stan, I apologize. I understood too late for Bob…I'd love having a second chance to speak with him!"
Stan laughs and says: "You're lucky, Lilly, Bob invited us for lunch today."
"That's so great! Merci! I won't drink. I promise."
I could never thank Stan enough. So this morning I look for information about P.A.J. Industries. It is French, no doubt. I consult my friend, Google: "headquarters, *Paris la Défense.*" They make plastic. I could write about plastic. *Pas de problème!*

Stan and I meet Bob at a restaurant that is supposedly chic but serves burgers.
"Bonjour Bob," I say, and then, in my best English accent, "Thank you so much for meeting with me again."
"*Bonjour,*" he says in good French, "Stan insisted."
For a French person, making a good impression while eating a burger with your hands is a real challenge. Plus, I'm really hungover. I try to chew and swallow as politely as possible. I take some of my French fries. Why are '*frites*' called 'French fries' in English? I'm pretty sure it's more of a Belgian thing? Whatever, I drink my Diet Coke with ice through a straw in silence. Stan tries to save me.

"Lilly did a very good job for us. And she's so friendly—everyone gets along with her. She's animated, motivated, and she speaks English well—this is too good for you to pass up! She's exactly what you've been looking for for months!" he says with a smile.

"Yeah… I can already think of several projects she would have been very helpful on," he replies.

Bob turns to me and says, "I'd like you to join my team, Aurelie. I'll put you in touch with our HR department if you're interested?" He hands me a card. "Contact her to arrange your visa, et cetera, ok?"

"*Merci!*" I exclaim. "Thank you so much! You won't regret it."

Bob leaves for a meeting nearby, and Stan offers me some cheese-cake to celebrate my new position. I'm so lucky!

From: LapetiteAurélieUSA
To: *"Poulettes"*
Subject: I'm coming back soon!

Mes poulettes,

I arrive on Monday at Charles de Gaulle. But good news: I might have a plan to go back to Philadelphia!
They have to check if it's possible for me to get a new visa but I think I found a new job! It's not for sure yet, so cross your fingers for me.

Otherwise, I have many surprises for you. I went to the outlets. I told you about these stores. They're cheaper, and they're a shopping paradise—it's like everything is on sale! I saved a ton, lol. I have a lot of jeans and other clothes for you!
I'm not writing you too long of an email 'cause I'm in a rush. I haven't finished packing yet!

Ok, for my birthday, the day of shopping in Paris sounds great. I miss you!

I also miss a good *Camembert* on a warm baguette and *un éclair au café* and *les croissants* and all the French food!

Aurélie

13. *Bienvenue à la maison* [1]

"Aurélie!" My mother's voice fills the entire house! I've just opened the door when I realize that it's been a while since I've heard my name pronounced so perfectly. *Je suis à la maison!* I'm back! Mom made all of my favorite meals. I eat *fromage de Neufchatel*, the best! And a mom stays a mom, so she says:
"So what are your plans now? What are you going to do? You need to find a job. With your Internet, you could have already begun."
"Véronique's daughter just found an excellent job. She found it on the Internet. And what about your birthday? Oh gosh—twenty-five! It makes me feel so old! How should we celebrate?"
"Surely you have plan with your friends… but your father and I thought you could do something with us…"
"Tomorrow you're starting a diet. You're not going to find a job like that…"
She kills me. I can't even find the strength to tell her that I'm pretty sure I already found a job in Philadelphia…

After four days at my parents' I want to leave. The day in Paris with my *poulettes* is wonderful. It feels like we were never apart. Caroline is freaking out because she just moved in with her *beau*. Stéphanie cut her hair short. She had always kept it very long, so she looks like a new girl to me! We laugh at my boyfriend stories from the U. S. I tell them about Jack again, the Brazilian guy, Jeff and his 8 hour drive, and of course, Tom and his Munchkins…
It is now official: I am Aurélie, a twenty-five year old with no job, who lives with her parents. But I am also Lilly who speaks fluent English.

1 Home sweet home

I check my e-mail inbox every hour. I look for one from P.A.J. Industries. I open an email from a "Lisa" :

From: Lisa Johnson <HumanResources, P.A.J. Industries>
To: Aurelie Jourdan
Subject: Communications Specialist position
> *Lilly:*
> *I am writing to offer you a two-year temporary position with the Communications department of PAJ Industries.*
> *You will report to Bob directly.*
> *We need to discuss the details of you local contract and our sponsorship of your work visa.*
> *Please contact me as soon as possible.*
> *Best regards,*
> *Lisa*

Yes!

*

Concorde station, the Parisian subway. I climb the stairs to a view of the famous *Obélisque* and the beginning of the *Champs-Elysées*. I walk to *Avenue Gabriel*, where the U.S. Embassy of Paris is located. I have bad memories of this place. Last year I spent three hours in line in this fortress. I expect the same thing today. I classify and arrange my documents, the DS156 I filled out online, the money order I got from the post office, the ID pictures—the American standard but without a smile—my job contract with PAJ, and the pre-stamped envelope for the return of my passport. I stand in line. My number is B 256. They call B 184. But this time, I know where I am going. I came with my *Elle* magazine. People jealously eye my magazine, as we wait for hours in this big room.
My turn! First checkpoint:
"Why would you like to go back to the U.S.?"
Many responses churn in my head. 'I have to go back because the man of my life is still waiting for me over there!' or 'I need to take a chance in Vegas, baby!'

Instead, I reply: "I'm going to work for a French company based in Philadelphia."

Bonne réponse! Good answer!

And three days later I receive my new E2 visa! This time, I have a one-year visa that is renewable once. That means I have two years to find my American boyfriend. And this time I already know the language, and I'll be working for a huge company. 400 employees. Surely I'll find one guy then, right?

My mom's response is one of confused disappointment:

"You couldn't find a job here so you need to go back there?" she says.

I frown.

"No, I am happy for you, obviously... If it's what you want..."

My *poulettes*, on the other hand, see themselves in a *Sex and the City* movie:

"Congratulations! Ok this time we'll visit you and we'll all go to New York."

"Next summer, we'll come, ok?"

"You only have ten days off at work?! Well you'll have to take at least five for us, ok?"

"This time you'll find him! Come on! You have two years! You'll find an American boyfriend, no doubt!"

*

To make a good impression on my first day at P.A.J. Industries, I decide to bring Bob some French delicatessen. What is most representative of our gastronomy than *foie gras*? So I prepare several nice assortments of *paté*, *saucisson*, and *foie gras*, and stash them in my carryon luggage. I prefer to keep an eye on them, because I'm scared someone will steal my gastronomic treasures.

And this time I take a huge bag with me. I'm going for two years! Two little bags are no longer enough. I need all my shoes, *bien sûr*. Knowing where I am going, the departure is less stressful. I called my landlord and my flat wasn't rebooked yet, so I'm going back to the same place: it's a good sign!

Paris, Charles de Gaulle Airport. My flight boards at 1:35 p.m. (for me, 13h35). Christmas Holidays are over! My new job begins next Monday, 11 a.m. I am in no hurry, and the E2 Terminal is full of *boutiques.* I say good-bye to my parents and my *poullettes.* I go to the security checkpoint. Laptop must come out, ok. Coat must come off, ok. Belt must come off . . . ok. Luckily I can keep my shoes on because I would really struggle to get them back on. If everyone had had an opportunity to see the aerobatic act I performed to get them on originally, I would be mortified. Last time I went through security here, a woman was crying because the guard threw away her Chanel mascara. Evidently mascara is a liquid within the confines of the Charles de Gaulle airport.

'Miss, could you come here please?" Says a guard. "I'm going to open your bag, ok?"

I follow her.

"What is this?" She asks, holding the cute little basket that I prepared for Bob in her hand.

"An assortment of French delicatessen," I reply, proudly.

"You can't enter the U.S. with it. I have to keep it. Sorry."

"Excuse me! No! Are you kidding? My friends told me it is ok to take foie gras!"

She stares at me with a blasé look. "Your friends were talking about cans of *Foie gras*, not fresh *foie gras* in a jar. Cans are ok, glass jars, no."

I immediately recognize what is going on. This lady wants my *Foie gras*! I can see her, staring at my jars of fresh, creamy, liver goodness, drooling. But, I will fight for my food. "Ok, so you're telling me I can't go through with this *foie gras*. Fine. But surely I can eat it over there by the window beforehand, right?'

"If you really want to," she replies, apathetically.

"Very well then," I say, shortly.

I accept this challenge. I sit down near the window, just across from the security line, and I open my *Foie gras* and dig in with a plastic fork I had brought from home. I'd rather get sick than let my precious, fresh delicacy rot in the trash, or even worse, to allow a stranger to savor it. Can, glass jar, what's the difference?

Ok, done. In retrospect, as I stand in the immigration line in the Philadelphia Airport, I do not recommend eating an entire can of *foie gras* right before a 7 hour flight. Just throw it away. I will spare you the details, but the flight was very painful.

I feel very confident arriving in Philadelphia—nothing like when I arrived in Boston. This time I know the process. I know where I am going, and I speak English. The officer waves me forward, and I give him my passport.

"What are you going to do in Philadelphia?" he asks, checking my papers.

"I'm going to work for P.A.J. Industries, a French company."

"But this is a student visa," he says, paging through my passport.

"Yes, but now I'm coming with a E2 Visa, on the next page, you see it?"

"Oh, ok. Enjoy your stay."

"Thank you."

I am so proud of myself. In the taxi, I say, in my best accent:

"22nd and the Benjamin Franklin Parkway, please!"

"Ok, miss," the driver replies.

No need for a little pink card made by my mother this time—victory!

14. *Intégration* [1]

First day at work. I'm as excited as I was on my first day back at school after summer break. My American boyfriend might be among the people I am going to meet today.

"No, miss. Without a badge, you can't go up there."

The security guy in the lobby of P.A.J. isn't joking. Apparently I can't take the elevator alone. I plead my case and he agrees to call the P.A.J. main reception desk.

"*Salut Aurélie!*"

I hear from behind me. Am I dreaming? It's not possible that an American could pronounce my name so perfectly.

"Bonjour," I say, turning my head.

In front of me is a very pretty girl, smiling, with blond, curly hair.

"Hey! I'm Claire," she says, "I'm a VIE at P.A.J. I've been here for 8 months! You'll see, it's a great place to work. You just arrived in Philly?"

"Hi! I'm so happy to meet you! I wasn't expecting to hear French today!"

"There are three French people here. With you, that makes 4 of us! Actually, there are more, but only 4 are young."

"Really? I thought I'd be the only French person. That's great!"

"There are sooo many French people in Philly," she says, amused. "When we have parties, we are usually like a hundred people."

"A hundred ... French people? I've been in the U.S. for a year and you're the first French person I've met."

"No way!"

Claire is surprised. So am I. She takes me to my cubicle and offers to meet me for lunch and bring along the other young French people.

---

1 Integrating

"Bonjour Lilly! Welcome!" Bob says, followed by 5 other new coworkers.

I'll let you settle in today, but tomorrow, there's a staff meeting at 9 a.m., ok?"

"Ok. Thank you!"

I don't have time to learn the other people's names before they disappear. An I.T. guy comes to set up my computer. I have a meeting with security to get my badge, and I have a "welcome to the company" meeting in the afternoon.

A maintenance worker stops by and hangs my name plate on the side of my cubicle.

The security guy who takes my badge picture carries a gun. I imagine him as Bruce Willis in *Die Hard* and wonder what he would do if our high rise were threatened by German terrorists…

*

For lunch, Claire introduces me to Thomas and Julien. We go out to the food court of a neighboring building called *Liberty Towers*. I have no idea how we got there. I just follow. P.A.J. Industries' headquarters is in the business area of Philadelphia—"center city"—on Market Street, between City Hall and 30th Street Station. The row of pristine high rises reflect off of each other's glass facades. One block south is Chestnut Street, one of the 2 main shopping streets in the city. We enter one Liberty Tower at the corner of 17th and Chestnut. I'm discovering a new world—the French expatriate world.

"You're a VIE too?" Thomas asks.

"What does VIE mean? Claire said the same thing, but I've never heard of it."

"It means Very Important Employee," says Julien, laughing.

"Come on guys! VIE stands for *Volontariat Interntional en Entreprise*, international volunteer job. We all have this status. We're here for a year or a year and a half with a J1 intern Visa. What about you?" says Claire.

"I signed a 2 year contract—an E2 work visa," I reply.

"2 years! That's great!" says Thomas, "but what kind of contract do you have?"

"Are you paid in dollars?" asks Julien.

"Yes. And they told me I get 10 days off. How do you survive with only ten days of vacation?" I ask, outraged.

"No way! You got screwed!" Julian laughs.

"It's just a different kind of contract," says Claire, reassuringly. "We're paid in Euros by the French government, so we get our normal five weeks vacation. You're on the U.S. system—ten days, that's tough…"

*

We go back to P.A.J., which takes up the top ten floors of the tower. My ears pop in the elevator on my way to the 36th floor. I hope this stops after awhile. Why do they work so high?

The afternoon surprises me more than I thought. The welcome meeting isn't an introduction to the company's product lines. No. It's a meeting about human relations. We are 3 new workers today. 2 women and 1 man. I am the only foreign person. Everyone is young—between 25 and 35. The Powerpoint is titled, *Sexual Harassment in the Workplace*. We would never have this kind of training in France! And I didn't have this kind of introduction at the Science History Association. A man from Human Resources gives us a card: 'In doubt? Call our confidential question line." I don't understand.

From: LapetiteAurélieUSA
To: "*Poulettes*"
Subject: A new world

Mes poulettes,
First day at work was very weird.
I met French people. What the hell? Do I care about French people? I want an American guy ;-(
Anyway, guess what, there's apparently a huge French community in Philly! I had no idea.
Then this afternoon I realized that the company won't help me to find a boyfriend.
I spent the afternoon listening to an ugly guy from HR lecture us on sexual harassment…no kidding.
Conclusion: if I find a man I like, he might sue me if I don't interest him? Come on!
Otherwise, I have my apartment back, I am so glad I live here again, and my friend Jenny is doing well.
Good to go! Round 2!
I will send you pictures of my place. I went with Jenny and her "honey" to Ikea. For 2 years, I prefer to invest in some actual furniture…
So my address hasn't changed! For the *Elle* magazines, same routine as last year, ok?
Merci mes amies!
Love,
Aurélie

15. *Une femme d'affaires* [1]

First thing's first. I am trying to learn all of my colleagues' names. Some of them invite me for lunch so we can get to know each other. This is my team! Alison, blonde, obese, with a kind of smiley demeanor. Mary, anorexic, always kind of hugging herself. Scott, nice mustache, but a biological profile to ensure a heart attack in the next hour. Then Maggie and Anna, a brunette and a redhead, both in their mid-fifties, both very traditional. Their reactions to my presence amuse me:

"You left your family to live here alone? Oh my God, hopefully my daughter will never do something like that!"

"I've never been to Europe. I've actually never left the U.S.!"

"You speak very good English!"

"You'll be very helpful in the department. Between you and me, I don't get a word of what some of our French workers say, even when they're speaking English!"

During my first month, I settle in. I proudly hang an Eiffel Tower post card my *poulettes* sent me in my cubicle. The Americans don't allow me much downtime, I'm always working. I am an American working woman! My work shoes sleep in my drawer and I wear tennis shoes to commute to and from the office, just like the American women here.

Living in New York, Yuriko has a lot of fun in her extended American student status. Being in the Big Apple is fantastic for an artist, the best... except for the cost of rent. So she has 4 roommates in a tiny apartment, she tells me. On the other hand, it didn't work out with Henri. She joins my *'I hate French guys'* club. We promise to visit each other soon. Just 2 hours by car separate us.

1 Working woman

This weekend I have plans with Jenny. She said she has big news, so I suggest we hit the nail salon we love, and I invite her and her boyfriend to a French party Claire told me about. When I meet her in front of our local Starbucks, she hugs me and jumps up and down:

"Lilly!" she says, taking my hands "he pro…blah blah blah!"

I think I recognize the word "propose," but I think I am missing a second meaning…

"What did he propose you to do?" I ask. Jenny is still for a moment, speechless, and then she says: "What?"

"What did he propose you?"

"Oh, Lilly! Come on! He proposed! That means he asked me to marry him!"

"*Oh mon Dieu!* Jenny! Sorry, I didn't understand like that! *Félicitations!* Congratulations! I am so happy for you guys!"

That's how I learned that "to propose" means many different things. She waves her left hand under my eyes. A huge diamond reflects Jenny's joy. My Jenny, she did it! She found her perfect American guy. Ok she is American, which is kind of an advantage, but still. She spills the details:

"We were at home, I wasn't expecting anything special!" she says. "He had made a candlelit dinner…"

Honey cooked dinner, I thought. Probably for the last time, I imagined.

"He did it after the dessert. We were on the couch, kissing…"

Do I have to listen to all the details, I think.

"And suddenly *Princess*, our cat, jumped on my knees…"

'There is a cat involved?,' I wonder to myself.

"And I saw it! Something was shinning on Princess' collar. My ring!"

He attached the engagement ring to the cat's neck? And she finds this romantic?

"Isn't that the cutest thing ever?"

Oh oui Jenny, your Honey is so cute…*Merveilleux*, wonderful! I feign interest.

We arrive at the French party, and I introduce Claire to Jenny and her boyfriend. They are really surprised to hear only French around them. I warned them! Tonight it's 100% French speaking! I meet mostly interns and VIE young people. It looks like we might be a hundred people packed into this tiny apartment. I'm 25, but it looks like I'm the oldest person here. But then I see someone who might be older than me.

"That's Philippe. He is an expatriate, but he's not married with kids or anything. He's a P.A.J. guy, too."

"I am an expatriate too," I say, "and I don't have a husband or kids!" The way she describes Philippe is a little strange to me.

"Yeah, but you're our age!" she says.

Oh bien sûr! True! I am closer to my twenties than this guy is, definitely!

"So why is he here?"

"He's Thomas's boss. He tells him about our parties to be nice, but usually Philippe never comes."

Philippe looks really bored—I see him take the last beer from the fridge and then discretely slip out of the apartment.

I learn that there are 3 big French companies in the area, so that's why there are so many French people. The 3 introduction questions are:

"Are you an intern or a VIE, and for which company?

"When did you arrive?"

"How long are you staying?"

After these 3 questions, no one seems to know what to say, but luckily you can spend all evening asking these questions to the one hundred guests.

Some are here for three or six months, but most of them are here for a year. Most of them also have only the dreaded "2 weeks vacation." One girl is visiting her boyfriend from France because he is doing his internship here. And Claire tells me all the gossip. Apparently this guy has two girlfriends in France—one came over Christmas break, and this one arrived later and has no idea. Smart, the *boulet!*

Claire points out another guy wearing a Phillies T-shirt. He just moved in with his American girlfriend! I can't believe it, this guy found his American girlfriend. 'Don't be so jealous,' Claire stops me. Everyone knows he doesn't want to stay here. He has to finish his school anyway. But he didn't tell her because she put her name on the lease. They had to sign for a year. And he's leaving in 5 months! Hopefully next party will be at their place: it's awesome!"

Many French guys ask me: *"C'est quoi ton téléphone?"* But I refuse to give *mon numéro* if the question isn't *"What's you number?"* from a cute American guy! Come on! I am not here to give my number to a French guy who will go back to France in 3 months!

*

French parties are great but they keep me away from my main goal of finding an American boyfriend. So I decide to risk it all. At work, Americans like to be part of a company team, like when they were back in college. They like sports competition and wearing a team T-shirt. At P.A.J., they have rowing, cycling, and running teams.

Rowing? To get oversized arms? And risk falling into the Schukyll River, which is no more appealing than The Seine River? No way.

Cycling? I don't have a bicycle in this country and I don't really like to bike. I always catch my heels on the pedals… my medical bills would be through the roof. No way.

Running? It seems really silly to run without a purpose? Well, this is a very American hobby. But I may have an obstacle with the extra weight that has appeared on my thighs. It's heavy to carry. Running would be hard, but it's my opportunity to meet the young American P.A.J. guys, and it would increase my chance to meet an athletic guy. I sign up.

I am filling out the papers when Scott, my colleague, pops his head into my cubicle and asks me to follow him:

"I have a job for you. I'd like you to work on an ad for one of our products."

I am glad to hear that. I have already worked on an ad for Alison. If Scott comes to me, it means Alison said something good about my work.

"Thank you Scott. For which product is it?" I say.

"For a glue!"

For a glue? Really?

"I'd like you to work on that project because it's for a French manager. Do you know a guy named Philippe?" He says.

"No. This name doesn't ring the bell…"

"Well the point is that you can speak French with him so you'll understand better than me what he wants for his ad."

"Ok."

"You'll make a French version and an English version of it, ok?"

This project seems really great. And working with a French guy? Easy for me! I make arrangements to meet this Philippe tomorrow morning.

*

As soon as I enter his office, I recognize Philippe. He is 'the old guy' from the French Party. He doesn't recognize me, so I don't mention it.

"*Bonjour*, call me Philippe."

He addresses me as "*vous*," our polite form of "you." The casual way is "*tu*." It surprises me. Come on! We are both French living in the U.S., a small group, even if we speak French, we can say "*tu*." It sounds better to me!

So I ask, "Maybe we can say "*tu*"—more casual, ok?"

"Yes, of course!" He says. "How long have you been working here?"

"I arrived 3 months ago."

"Are you an intern or a VIE?"

He kills me, thinking I could be an intern. Do I look that young?

"No," I say. "I'm a real employee. I lived in the U.S. for a year before I got this job!"

"Oh really?" He says.

"Yes really. And what about you? Are you an intern or a VIE?" I smile.

"No I am not either. I am an expatriate. I've been working for the company for almost 8 years. I began in Paris and they sent me to

107

China for three years, then back to Paris and then here. I arrived 3 months ago, like you."

"Great! I signed for 2 years, you?"

"I signed for 3 years. I did the same amount of time in China…"

"I bet China was amazing, right? Do you speak Chinese?"

"It was a very good experience. I do speak Mandarin, I mean enough to find my way!"

"Tell me where are you living?"

"Well, aren't we here to work on an ad?"

It would have been more fun to talk about his time in China, but he doesn't seem eager to do that. He is very chatty though about his expectations regarding his glue ad…

"Ok, so when I've finished the ad, I'll check with Scott and then send you a proof, ok?"

"Great!"

"*Au revoir* then. Maybe I'll see you around at the next French Party?"

"I don't think so. I'm not a student anymore! I actually spend like at least a quarter of my time in Paris, when I'm not in Asia…I'm not often in Philadelphia…"

From: LapetiteAurélieUSA
To: *"Poulettes"*
Subject: Run Forrest Run!

Salut my "French Chickens?"
Everything is going well on my side of the ocean.
We had many days off for snow. "Snow days." Yeah, it's been snowing a lot since early March. For almost a month now I've been wearing my UGGs to walk to the office!
And when it snows a lot during the day, the office closes at 3 p.m. Soooo great!
See in the picture I sent you how peaceful the city is under the snow?
Winter is hard though but soon this season will be over and I'll complain because it's too hot!

News of the year: I'm becoming a runner! I can hear you laughing...
Here is my reasoning: At work there are sports teams. Who joins sport teams? Hot, athletic guys, *bien sûr*! So, to meet my American boyfriend, I have to join a team!
By process of elimination, I joined the running team!
It begins in April. We meet 2 times a week at 5 p.m. and we run together. The goal is to run The Philadelphia Half Marathon in November with the company T-shirt.
With the body of a runner, I increase my chances!

Aurélie
PS: When are you coming to visit me?

16. *Se faire belle* [1]

Monday evening. *Gossip Girls* is on. I'm eating Oreo cookies. One more week and the running training begins. I received my official team T-shirt at the office. Our motto is: 'Run, P.A.J. Industries! Run!' I've been back in Philly for three months, and not one American guy has hit on me... And I haven't even been attracted to any American guy... Which is worse?

My phone rings. No way! Who dares to bother me on a Monday evening? I glance at my phone. It's Jenny. I pick up:

"*Bonsoir* Jenny..."

"Hey! Lilly, I know it's Gossip Girls time... but it's on commercial break, I checked! This will just take a sec, ok?"

"Yeah..."

"Are you sitting down?"

I am on the couch, enveloped in my pajamas and a blanket.

"Ok, how does sunny Las Vegas sound to you?"

"What? Las Vegas, the slot machine place?"

"Yep! Vegas! My sis, cousin and best friend just called and they're planning a weekend in Vegas to celebrate my engagement! Like an early bachelorette party!"

"A *batch*...what?"

"New word, Lilly! A good one! In the U.S., a few weeks before the wedding, the bride goes out for a big night with her girlfriends, and the groom does the same with his buddies..."

"Oh! *Oui, bien sûr!* In French we say '*Enterrement de vie de jeune fille*' meaning literally 'funeral of your single life!' I see!"

1 Looking good

"A funeral?! French people are so weird… Anyway… You know my family and childhood friends live in San Francisco. So my girl-friends think it would be fun to meet kind of half way! You wanna come?"

I didn't remember that Jenny was from San Francisco, but a bach-elorette party, with just girls and a lot of alcohol, and in Vegas on top of that!?

"Of course Jenny! I'd love to come with you!"

After I hung up, I jumped on my bed and threw the Oreos away!

*

At work, everything is going smoothly. Claire is cute and a lot of fun to be around. Sometimes we call each other 40 times a day on the internal P.A.J. Industries line, and we have lunch together every day. Everything is going well.

Today is my first day of running training. I am so excited to meet the fit, athletic guys of the company. I can't focus all day. Eventu-ally, at 5 p.m. I head down to the lobby, the meeting point. Then, I see our "team." I immediately want to turn back. They are all wearing tight, elastic running gear. I am the only one wearing the P. A.J. T-shirt. They're examining each other's watches and talking about "cardio." I have no idea what they are talking about, and I quickly realize that none of them is under 40. Where are the young guys? Come on! The women stare at me with the international look of 'I'm fitter than you.' I overhear them:

"Oh my God, is that last year's New York marathon T-shirt?!

"Yes! It was such an amazing run."

"What was your time?"

"Four hours two minutes!"

"Congratulations! I did my last one in four seventeen."

Oh mon Dieu, I have to get out of here… They run marathons? I am just here to meet a good-looking guy. I see none, so all I have to do is return to my office, change, head home, and disappear into my bed. I'm about to stealthily return to the elevator, when I hear:

"Hey, are you coming with us? What's your name?"

Merde…

"Hi…I'm Lilly…from the communications department…"

"Hi! I'm Sam and this is Sandra."

I could identify every one of Sandra's muscles—the best legs I have ever seen.

"Nice to meet you. I think I'm going to run alone before joining you guys…"

"No no! Bad idea," Sam replies, with a kind of abrupt tone. Then she announces to the group:

"Welcome P.A.J. Industries runners! I'm the coach, Sam. I know most of you from last year! Today we'll begin with a 5-mile run, ok? We'll follow the Schuylkill for a bit and then come back, ok? Ready?"

Five miles!? I'm trying to figure out what that is in kilometers, when I hear a new voice.

"Wait guys! Sorry I'm late! I'd love to join you, if it's ok?" says a male voice as he exits the elevator. This guys looks like the others—an American runner with a tiny T-shirt, but his accent is French. Wait, is that Philippe?

Ok let's go! We run. Very quickly, everyone is ahead of me. I try to mimic the others' leg movements as best I can from the rear. The trail following the river would have been nice—at a leisurely pace. But now I have the feeling that I am spitting out my lungs, and my watch shows that we've only been at this for ten minutes. Does time pass more slowly while running? Sam, as a good coach, checks on me.

"You're doing great! Keep it up!"

I am as red as a cosmo, and I'm sweating like I am at a rock concert. I can't even answer her. She sees I'm feeling faint and suggests:

"Hey, maybe you should run for a minute thirty, then walk for a minute. You got a chronometer?"

She looks skeptically at my watch, and then rejoins the others. My lace bra is killing me. I'm dripping with sweat. How could I be so out of shape?

Philippe joins me:

"*Salut Aurélie!* Sam asked me to cheer up the French girl in the back! I didn't know it was you!"

Oh God, can he please just go away? I'm dying back here. I don't need an audience.

"Philippe! You run?"

"I love it! I've been running for years. I did the New York marathon 3 years ago!"

Is he kidding me? He does look like an egghead…what a pain in the ass, this guy. The sweat is running down on my face, and I need to blow my nose, but I don't have a tissue… Philippe offers me one from a hidden pocket in his magic T-shirt… I stop to use it when the rest of the team turns around to go back to the office.

The end never comes. I think I've been running/walking/crawling forever. Philippe runs to the front. I am the last one to arrive at the tower lobby. They are all still stretching and smiling at me as I go directly to the elevator: "Well done, Lilly!" I feel absolutely awful. I don't want to hear their ridiculous cheering. I just joined to meet Matthew McConaughey and become his devoted wife. But now I'm humiliated, and in front of a bunch of marathon runners, no less. Luckily, there was no potential American boyfriend to see this. Shame on me! *La honte…* I have never felt so ugly.

It's hard to go back home on foot. After a bath, I Google 'miles to kilometers.' So 1 mile is *1.6 kilomètre*. I ran 8 km! Well, not exactly… I look at myself in the mirror; it's time to react! I've put on some weight since I moved to the U.S. What can I do?

I Google '*régime*'—diet. Who is Jenny Craig? Is she famous? She says that I can "lose 20 lbs for $20." What the hell does "lbs" stand for? I continue reading about American diets and eventually figure out that it means "pounds," obviously. So one pound is 0.4536 kilogram. Easy to convert… I would like to lose 5 kilos, so that's 11.0229 pounds. I want to cry…

A Weight Watchers ad pops up on my screen. "Ready to lose weight?" It asks. Ready? Me? *Oui oui…* I click on "find a meeting" and enter my zip code. I can't believe it—in my area alone, there are 5 sites. They're everywhere… So I start to see it as an American experience. Losing weight here is like being part of the community. I'll learn a lot, and meet new American people. Ok, I commit to go next Wednesday at 5:15 p.m, 1500 Walnut Street.

By running 2 times a week and going to Weight Watchers, I should lose my extra pounds before my *poulettes* visit me. Just by logging onto the website, I feel like I've already lost weight.

*

"Are you kidding me? You're going to Weight Watchers?" Claire laughs out loud.

"Don't tell anyone! Ok?" I don't want the whole French community to know.

"Why are you doing that?"

"I don't want to become obese!" I share my fear, as I sip my skim milk Starbucks coffee in front of P.A.J.

"Ok, but you're nuts, Aurélie! Anyway, there's a party this weekend for Julien's departure. He's been here for a year, so his VIE ends this month."

"I'll come!"

"I heard that next month a new French guy is joining the Finance department. Hopefully he'll be as nice as Julien…" we giggle.

Then, more seriously, Claire says:

"It's weird to see people arriving and leaving so quickly… This summer there will be a going away party almost every weekend for the people who have been here 18 months… I did the opposite—I arrived in June, so I'll leave this Christmas…"

"It will go fast…"

"You're going to witness a lot of French employee turnover in the two years you are here."

She's right, it's strange to see people come and go so quickly. I'll be sad to see Claire go in December, but saying goodbye to Julien won't hurt me at all!

Before joining the team this week, I get some new athletic gear. I don't want to embarrass myself again. I buy *Runner* magazine. "Running—It's in your mind," I read. And I can only focus my mind if I'm well dressed. I read the article on the 10 best shoes. $95 for shoes without heels?! I'm heartbroken. What am I doing? This country is changing me... So I choose the blue shoes, with the little turquoise design on the side. I learn from *Runner* magazine about something called a "sports bra." They recommend that we wear these during our runs. No kidding? They are not sexy, but they seem more comfortable than lace, so I believe the article. On Thursday, they are so surprised to see me at the P.A.J. runner team meeting. Sam is pleased:

"Lilly! Nice! You're hanging in there!"

"*Merci*! I wear the good shoes this time, see?" I display my feet proudly.

"Ok. Let's go, team!" she says.

I feel better, but I certainly don't run any faster than last week. I may have pushed myself a little too hard this week, because as soon as I get home I throw up. But I am so proud of myself. I am even more excited thinking of my first Weight Watchers meeting.

The following Wednesday, I walk to 1500 Walnut Street for my first meeting. I am stopped as soon as I get out of the elevator. There's a line to enter the room that stretches down the entire hallway. All the way down to the end, I see women disappear, one after the other, into the room. 20 minutes later, I reach the door. We are still queuing in the room where I see many rows of chairs. And a scale! The line ends at a scale! First, you pay 14 dollars to enter the room. Then you get on the scale. After that, you can sit and wait for everyone to be weighed. I see women taking off their bracelets, their shirt, shoes, hair bands... everything that can make you fatter?

"Hi! It's my first time!" I say to the woman seated at the small desk near the scale. She is the one that records your weight in your notebook.

"Hi! Step onto the scale."

Ok! I do. *La balance*, the scale, doesn't speak French. I try not to cry seeing a lot more than a 100. It's in pounds not kilos, I tell myself. Don't panic! The woman doesn't even notice my anxiety. She jots down the number and adds her stamp.

After she has weighed everyone, she stands up and takes her place at a small podium at the front of the room. "Hello everyone!"
And everyone answers in unison: "Hello!"
She begins: "My name is Lucy, and I lost 52 pounds on the Weight Watchers program!"
The crowd, at least 60 people, applauds energetically.
"Let's welcome our new members today."
"Welcome," says the crowd.
"I'll let them introduce themselves…"
Oh non, I have to speak in front of all these people. No way. A blond girl stands up:
"Hi! I'm Katie. I gave birth to my second child 6 months ago and I just can't lose all the baby weight…"
"Welcome Katie!" says the crowd.
Ok I have to say at least a few words. I'm here conducting an undercover investigation to understand more about American culture. I have to do it.
"*Bonjour*! Hi! I'm Lilly. I come from France. I arrived in the U.S. a year and a half ago. Food is very different here and I gained 11 pounds not even realizing it…"
"Welcome Lilly!" says the crowd.
Nice. Then everyone exchanges tips and shares their frustration with dieting. I get a list of food and their "value" in Weight Watchers points. I am allowed to eat 20 points a day. Ok, I get the idea. The atmosphere is great. No one is judgemental, and I think it's so funny that the crowd applauds every time someone speaks. Such a good feeling!

From: LapetiteAurélieUSA
To: *"Poulettes"*
Subject: I love running. I do!

You're not going to believe me! I'm a runner! Hopefully you'll recognize me!

I'm so happy you can come. August 15 sounds perfect! I'll take some days off to go with you to New York.
I'll take care of everything, ok? You just have to come! I'll find us a not too expensive hotel in Manhattan.

Cross your fingers for me this weekend: you have to bring me luck! I'm going to Las Vegas! If I find myself lucky enough I might win at the slot machines or get married to Ashton Kutcher's lookalike lol

Miss you,
XOXO
Lilly

17. *Les folies de Las Vegas* [1]

Tonight I fly to Las Vegas, Nevada. Claire is so jealous! My morning goes quickly. Now I just have a 2 p.m. meeting with Philippe, and then I leave for Vegas. Speak of the devil, here comes Philippe. It's 1:30 p.m.

"*Salut Aurélie.*"

"*Salut?*"

"I'm not interrupting you or anything?"

I click on a Word document to cover up that I'm looking at *Viedemerde.com* – a crazy French website where people talk about their misfortunes. It's hilarious.

"No obviously, come on in!"

"Aurélie, could we postpone our meeting to Monday? I'm a little busy today."

"Sorry, that's not going to be possible on Monday! I'm leaving for Vegas tonight. I'll be back on Tuesday if you want?"

"Nice! You're spending the weekend in Vegas? I heard it's a once-in-a-lifetime experience! You're going with some friends?"

"Yeah! It's a girls-only weekend."

I point to my suitcase, all ready to go in the corner of my cubicle, and a Vegas guide on my desk. He smiles and takes out his Blackberry:

"Let me check when we can meet on Tuesday... Let see...3 p.m.?"

"Ok!"

"By the way, I'd like to ask you for some help?"

"Sure, what's going on?"

1 Las Vegas craziness

"It's for a friend, a very good friend from college, a wonderful girl. Her company is sending her here. World is small isn't it? Well, she asked me for some advice to find a place downtown…"

"Great…"

"Yes, you see when I moved here, a real estate agent was assigned to help me. So how did you find your apartment?"

I hesitate a second and then… I had the misfortune of finding an alcoholic roommate, but it does work for others… And I bet he'll visit the apartments with her. So I say:

"I looked on Craigslist, on the internet. I am sure it will help your friend."

"Thank you! It's nice of you. I am looking forward to seeing her."

I could care less about this girl! But if we don't have to meet, it means I can leave early for Vegas! Let's go to Vegas!

*

We have just landed in Vegas, and I wake up to a magical world. I can't believe what I hear. Not far from the plane, while the engines are still making noise, I can hear the dreamy sound of money falling from the slot machines! What a lovely melody! I am in the baggage claim area. I am not hallucinating: rows of slot machines are lined up as far as the eye can see. Along the walls, my eyes are attracted to many sparkling ads announcing the different shows you can see here. *Le Cirque du Soleil*, Céline Dion, Tom Jones, even Elton John! Each ad is more brightly lit than the next. They make me dizzy! And the marvelous sound of the slot machines tinkle in my head.

"Jenny, I love Las Vegas!"

"Lilly, you're still in the airport!" she says, amused by my enthusiasm.

Jenny has already been there several times. She explains that Vegas is the perfect place for every American to celebrate their 21st birthday, the legal drinking age, because Vegas always has perfect party weather: hot and sunny, in the middle of the desert.

It's 10 p.m. local time and, despite the 3-hour time difference, I am not tired at all. We take a cab: "Caesar's Palace, please!" We drive through the Strip, the main avenue of the city. All the most extravagant hotel casinos are on this road. I see the Eiffel Tower! I am not kidding. A little further away, there's the Statue of Liberty with a roller coaster right behind it. Then, a fortified castle, and a pyramid… My eyes jump out of their sockets! This place is extraordinary. It's daylight during the night as the buildings light up and reflect each other's brightness from every part of the Strip.

In the lobby of our temple, we are immersed in a roman atmosphere, columns, and statues all over. The hotel entrance is through the casino. The hotel's lobby is also the casino. Or maybe it's the other way around. Perhaps we are in a casino where you also can rent hotel rooms.

We walk through a field of slot machines to get to the elevators. Jenny explains:

"My sister Carol, my cousin Christina, and Amy, my best friend, will arrive in a bit. I'm looking forward to introducing you!"

She keeps on talking about their friendship, telling me anecdotes, etc., but I can't concentrate. The gambling tables and shiny décor mesmerize me. Jenny grabs my arm and we head up to our room, which just elevates the level of craziness of this casino. We booked 2 adjoining rooms. With the rococo style and the view on the Strip, we feel like we're already in a club!

Jenny and I begin to change while waiting for the others. I'm trying to look like a Las Vegas 'pin up' girl, so I select a sequined red dress. As they say, it's a once-in-a-lifetime experience! I put on my sexy, glimmering dress, and Jenny is gorgeous in a backless white dress. I am in the middle of my make up step when I realize something very strange in the bathroom:

"Jenny! Come in here! There's a TV in the bathroom!"

She laughs: "I know! It's Vegas, Lilly! Everything's crazy here!"

Ok but still, there's a TV on the bathroom. I take a picture because otherwise my *poulettes* will never believe me. Then a huge eruption of noise jolts me.

"Ooooooh… my… God! Let's seeeeeeeeeeeee your ring! Oooooooooh my God! You're going to get maaaaaaaaarried!"

They hug each other and cry and smile and laugh… Then comes the introduction:

"Is this your French friend?" Asks Jenny's sister, holding out her hand to me. I guess I am the extra attraction of the weekend!

"Hi! Nice to meet you!"

"Ready to party like an American girl?" Says the cousin, kissing me on the cheeks. "I saw that French people say hi like this on TV!"

I smile. Amy does the same. Doing *la bise* makes them laugh, go figure!

Carole is the most touched by the situation:

"I can't believe my little sis is getting married!"

Jenny and Carol have the same face shape and the same pointed chin. I instantly feel the similarity that links all of them. I am flattered that Jenny invited me to share these intimate moments.

All dolled up, the 5 of us finally get to the bar. 5 Cosmopolitans, please! And let's try these slot machines! You have to find the one for you. Some take one penny per bet, or a quarter, a dollar, 2 dollars, and in a private room we see some that are 5 dollars per bet. Just imagining losing 5 bucks each time I push the big red button scares me! We decide that a quarter per bet is already a lot, so we sit in a row and cheer Jenny!

$15 later, a cute waitress in a sexy, and very small, toga comes and asks us what we are drinking. We order 5 more cosmos, *bien sûr!* And we're back in the game! When she comes back with our drinks I open my little red handbag – that matches my dress - and say to the girls:

"This round is on me! I'm so happy to share this weekend with you! Thank you!"

They all laugh in one voice, the waitress too. She gives us our drinks and leaves, winking at the girls. Jenny comes to me and says:

"Lilly, you're cute, thanks. I should have told you, in Vegas when you gamble, alcohol is free!"

What? Happy Las Vegas!

The next morning—well, the next afternoon—I open one eye. I still have my make up on. As hard as it is, I manage to open both eyes and I realize that I am not alone in bed. We are all together, the five of us, passed out on the same bed…in our clothes…thank God. Too many cosmos… My first thought is, "please, I hope I didn't lose too much money on the slot machines… or at the roulette table." Images of black and red numbers run through my mind. It's not very clear, but I don't remember anyone hitting the jackpot. I push off the stray arm laid across me and find my way out of bed. I go directly for my handbag. My credit card is there—a good sign.

After our showers, we put on our bikinis. Apparently the cure for a Las Vegas hangover is a strawberry margarita by the pool! What else? As soon as Jenny plunges into the antique-decorated pool, Carol whispers to all of us:

"Everything is planned for tonight! Tonight's the big night!"

Tonight is the 'big night'? What was yesterday all about? I think I already gave my best. Today I'm exhausted. Jenny leans closer and says:

"What's going on here?"

"Nothing! It's a surprise!" says Carol.

Jenny understands she won't have much more information so she goes back to swimming for a while. We encircle Carol and she can't resist telling us:

"I booked a table at the Chippendales show tonight!"

Oh oui! Chippendales? We are going to watch handsome, athletic guys get undressed for us! I love American bachelorette parties!

*

At 5 p.m. I have already tasted the Caesar's special coconut cocktail and I am sunburned on both sides. We decide to visit the Strip. *Oui*, you can "visit" Las Vegas. The idea is to have one drink in as many Casinos as you can enter. So we try. The third Casino we enter is the Venetian. This one is particularly attractive to us, and we settle into one of the many bars. The Venetian is a true reproduction of the most famous monuments of Venice. It's baffling. Everything is smaller but I feel the color and atmosphere of Italy. We smell the sugary taste of Italian ice cream walking through the little Saint Marc Place. Lovers can take a tour in a gondola on the Grand Canal—it's even the same color... We all have a little too much to drink, so the romantic atmosphere makes us nostalgic.

"Lilly, do you have a boyfriend?" Carol asks, as we walk on the Rialto Bridge.

"Well no... No one is waiting for me here or in Paris. I'm out there though. I am. American guys don't want me..."

"I'm single too... I can't believe my little sis is getting married before me..."

"Come on, Carol, I know Mark wanted to marry you, but he was a jerk," says Jenny, "I hope you dumped him for good this time!"

Carol spent six years with a *boulet* that she finally managed to leave three months ago. We can all tell that she is not over him yet, but from what I've heard from the others, it sounds like she made the right move. Amy diverts the conversation:

"Harry broke up with me..."

"What happened, sweetie?"

"Well, I was super-bored at one of his business events, and I couldn't help flirting with one of his coworkers. He wasn't amused."

Carol laughs:

"You're the best, Amy! How long did you stay with this one? 4 months? That breaks your three-month record, no?"

Now that Amy's story is taken care of, they focus on me. Christina is feeling very concerned, she stares at me like she's trying to take in my "dating" aura:

"I don't understand why you're single. You're French, they should hit on you just for your accent!"

She's being sincere, but if she wants explanation, I'm going to give her my opinion on American guys:

"Ok, so I met a cute blond guy who drove eight hours to take me to a fancy restaurant, then never called me back. Another one had a girlfriend but he swore to me it wasn't a problem because they were

living in "Munchkin land." Since then I'm lost. The cultural difference may be too heavy…"
The girls laugh. I can't be upset at them. I'm pathetic. Amy asks:
"And at work? Have you met anyone interesting? I know I met
some great guys at work. Identify the ones who always stay late, it
means they are single!"
"At work? Honestly I did try there too. I joined the running team
hoping to meet a guy."
Confessing that I am so desperate that I joined the running team to
meet guys makes them aware of my situation. They stop laughing.
Jenny changes the subject—either to come to my rescue or just to
end this dead-end conversation:
"Come on! Ok you're all single now. But I love you! I'm not worried for you because I know you'll meet the perfect guy—just like I
met my honey!"
"Jenny we're sorry. We didn't want to screw up your day! We'll
stop complaining about our love lives, we promise!"
We force ourselves to smile, and five cosmos later our nostalgic
moment is over. Let's have some fun! *C'est la fête à Las Vegas!*

*

The girls have everything under control for tonight. They have a
tiara for Jenny, the queen of the evening! A table is booked under
her name, and a bottle of champagne is ready to pop! The atmosphere of the club isn't as creepy as I thought it would be. It's only
women—overly excited, yes—but in a fun way. Mostly bachelorette parties! The waiters wear red thongs, and we dare Jenny to put
a rolled-up one-dollar bill in the waiter's thong… with her
month… Since I don't have to play, it's fun.
Several drinks in a row and three Tequila shots, I feel good here! I
blame these three shots for the rest of the X-rated evening. Carol
leaves the table a moment. When she comes back, she is so happy
to share:
"I did it!" I guess she didn't go to the restroom. I don't understand
what she did though. But Amy has an idea. She is the only one who
reacts:

"Please tell me you didn't! Not to Jenny!"

"Come on!" says Carol. "It'll be fun!"

"You think so?"

I am leering at the ass of one of the waiters, so I know I missed a part of the conversation but I don't really care. What a mistake on my part. The girls realize that I didn't understand:

"I booked a show for Jenny! They're going to pull her on stage!"

I see they are excited but I am not sure why. I'm puzzled. What's going to happen to my Jenny? The stage is for the strippers. Why would she go up there? Amy realizes that I still don't have a clue. She explains, gesturing toward the stage where the curtain opens:

"See, after the show, they ask some girls from the audience to come on stage. Carol put Jenny's name on the list to be called. You get it?"

The curtain opens and reveals five gorgeous guys, to die for, in fire-men suits. Apparently this is an international fantasy. They begin to dance—well, strip. Then handsome guys start falling from the sky, in doctor's jackets, police uniforms, construction outfits, and army uniforms… Amy takes a picture to prove that we are all so into the show. I almost forget that a surprise is waiting for my Jenny… She applauds and drinks without suspicion. The show ends to a stand-ing ovation. Actually, these guys do deserve it.

The end of the show? Not exactly! The curtain opens up again to five empty chairs lined up on the stage. A cute tattooed guy takes the microphone and calls the five lucky girls. Jenny is sipping what must be her seventh drink of the evening and almost has a heart attack when she hears her name. She turns to Carol:

"You didn't! Please tell me they are calling another Jenny!"

The girls stand up, applauding, so I stand up too. I smile at Jenny. Carol brings her up to the stage. I'm not really sure what's going on, but Jenny doesn't seem too happy. Four excited girls take their chairs on the stage, but Jenny looks mortified.

Behind them, in tempo with the music, five marvelous guys arrive. A cute one grabs Jenny by her hips and yeah! He turns her around until she ends up head down, feet up! My heart stops for her. In one movement, he lays her onto the floor and gets on top of her, mimicking interesting things... It's been so long, I hope I still remember how that works. He moves his hips for a long time then makes one more turn and carries her over his shoulder and puts her back on her chair.

Ok I want to be her. No no no, just kidding…!

I keep my eyes wide open to memorize the order of what I just witnessed. I am immobile as the others dance. Well, I guess it's my first time!

When we get our Jenny back, she arrives with surprises for each of us. One of the "policeman" dancers takes cares of me. I would have never thought I would do something like this and fully intend to deny that I did. Oh the price of partying with American girls!

*

We sleep by the pool the entire next day. The girls make fun of me for being kind of ashamed of what we did last night and Amy says: "We Americans have a motto for Las Vegas: whatever happens in Vegas, stays in Vegas! So don't worry, Frenchie!"

I don't feel like writing that to my *poulettes*. They would not understand.

18. *Rumeur au travail* [1]

This Tuesday morning it's especially hard to concentrate on Philippe's glue ad. Very hard. Running tonight seems completely impossible and going to Weight Watchers tomorrow is like preparing for a meeting with the devil. If I sum up 2 points per alcoholic drinks this past weekend, I think I used all my points for the entire weekend before I even had my first meal. It's going to be a long week.

Connecting to my work e-mail, I see a company-wide invite to do volunteer work for a charity organization. "Join the P.A.J. Industry Project, help rebuild your community." Help? Me? I'm always happy to help anyone, but I don't see the link with the company. In these kind of situations, I always find answers with Alison. She is always a good adviser.

"United Way is a well-known charity in the U.S."

"What does P.A.J. do for them?"

"They do this every year—they let us volunteer one day per year during normal work hours—sometimes it's painting or cleaning. And they organize games to raise money in the cafeteria."

"I'd like to help too!"

"That's great, Lilly. It's a lot of fun and it's wonderful feeling like you're a part of something good."

"What can I do?"

"I heard this year that Kelly is going to organize a smoothie party and a mini-golf game. Give her a call—see what you can do."

A smoothie party? Mini golf? That arouses my curiosity. I sign up Claire, Thomas, and myself. Together, we go together to Kelly's desk.

1 Work gossip

"I'm so happy to see French people concerned for the Philadelphia community!" she says, welcoming us. "The more the merrier!"

She puts us in charge of getting T-shirts. Every employee who gives money or volunteers will get a T-shirt. At Weight Watchers, I wore the lightest outfit, shoes, and accessories that I could find, but it didn't cover the truth. I gained four pounds over the weekend. Going to a Weight Watchers meeting having gained weight is a terrible experience. No one applauded me.

*

Smoothie Party day is here. Or should I say, the first fundraising event for the United Way is today. From 11 a.m. to 1 p.m., smoothies, along with other treats, are served in the 38th floor cafeteria. The head manager from each department serves the smoothies. They all wear cute aprons and take their job very seriously. Bob, my boss, offers me a strawberry banana smoothie. It's a huge success.

The next morning in the cafeteria, a graduated thermometer is drawn on a panel. A caption explains that if we raise 10 % more than last year, we can wear jeans to the office for the last three Fridays in June. Kelly and the rest of the team are very optimistic. The mini-golf party should do it. We are so looking forward to next week.

*

This weekend I can't take it anymore—I boycott the Saturday night French party. Jenny is busy planning her wedding, but she doesn't need my help at this point. I see only one thing to do: lock myself in my apartment. I turn off Skype, close Facebook, and buy enough junk food to satisfy my hunger and thirst for the entire weekend (how many points is an entire quart of chocolate Ben and Jerry's? Ideas?). I rent some DVDs: *Le marriage de mon meilleur ami* (My Best Friend's Wedding), *La guerre des mariées* (Bride Wars), *Le témoin amoureux* (Maid of Honor), *27 robes* (27 Dresses), *Sexe and the City*

1&2 (Sex and the City—the movie and the sequel). That should tide me over until Monday.

Next week, golf club in the hand, I sport my P.A.J. Industries United Way T-shirt. I host the second fundraising. We installed three golf holes in the cafeteria. Kelly checks the donation box— donations are flowing! I hope to meet every employee. I hand the golf club to Philippe, who follows me with a huge smile. I assume my hostess role and explain the rules:
"If you do well, you can win a P.A.J. Industries pen." I show him how to assume the correct golfing position.
"Merci! I'm impressed," he says.
I don't know how many people I passed the golf club to, but my cheeks hurt from my permanent smile.
Once the game is over, we have to clean up. Kelly thanks us a hundred times before going back to work. It's just the three of us, *les Français*, putting the tables back in place. Claire laughs:
"I saw you talking to Philippe... do you know him well?"
"I worked with him on an ad."
"You seem to get along very well..." She says, with a playful smile.
Before I can reply, Thomas interjects:
"Don't waste your time with that guy! He's gay."
"Really?" I did not see that coming.
"Yeah—one of my friends from Paris told me."
"Are you sure?" I'm surprised. "Last time he talked to me about an old college friend coming to Philly to visit... he seemed really close to her..."
"A shopping friend, I guess!" says Thomas.
I don't think Thomas is right, but I don't really care. And that's enough to quell Claire's teasing.
At the end of the day—mission accomplished. We raised more money this year than last year, so we're allowed to wear jeans in June. *Quelle chance!* Awesome!
We're proud to have done a good job fundraising, and we all applied for the 'off site' volunteer day too.
The following week, instead of going to work on Monday, the

P.A.J. Industries employees' goal is to help fix up a school in South Philly. We are offered two possible activities: landscaping or painting. Claire, Thomas, and I choose to paint. We clean the walls and then paint them with great motivation. Almost a hundred employees are wearing their T-shirts today. The atmosphere is casual, but we are serious about our work. After 6 hours, we are dirty and tired but happy, and the school looks good again.

Isn't that the American spirit?

From: LapetiteAurélieUSA
To: *"Poulettes"*
Subject: *Je suis toujours là!* I'm still here.

Sorry my *poulettes*, I haven't given you any news for a while now.
Here are my updates, in order:
Las Vegas was more than awesome! I'll send you the pictures. Me
in front of the slot machines, me by the pool, and me in the bathroom to show you there's a TV! *C'est fou!* It was crazy!
And more recently, I took part in a volunteer program (United
Way) through work, where I helped to paint a school in a needy
area of Philly. I'll send you more pictures: me with a brush, me
wearing my United Way T-shirt...

Also, as you will see, *oui*, I gained more weight. The cheeseburgers
won! But I'm fighting back. I'm going to Weight Watchers.
Being on a diet in the country of fat domination is like torture in
the Middle Ages.
How can I resist chocolate chip cookies, carrot cake, cheesecake,
milkshakes, brownies, sundaes, muffins, scones, and donuts...?
How?

Aurélie, still looking for her American boyfriend but running into
obstacles

19. *Mac contre PC* [1]

Summer. It's too hot to work, let alone run. June is organized around my running club training and Weight Watchers meetings. I eventually lose a few pounds, and my *poulettes* arrive in 6 weeks. I am looking forward to showing them Philadelphia.

As I lose weight, I start to feel better. Surfing on a wave of happiness, Claire succeeds in twisting my arm to go with her to a singles party.

Claire is recovering from a break up with a French guy and she knows I'm looking for an American guy. She wants to have fun. Why not? Jenny encourages me to go. She tells me singles parties are common in the U.S. And I will obviously have a great evening with Claire. Ok, my Saturday night is booked.

Our American boyfriends will wait for us in a bar in Manayunk—a cute little area, very close to center city, accessible by the local R6 train. I have never been to a singles party, but I can't say that my American boyfriend will appear by himself, so why shouldn't I make the first move? I do feel more and more like an American girl these days. If women go to single parties here, I can too. How could I not attract an American guy feeling so much like an American girl?

As I leave my favorite store, Anthropologie, with the cute new dress I bought to celebrate my weight loss, I grab a Starbucks coffee to go and walk along the parkway in my flip-flops, coffee cup in my hand, I feel so American! *Oui.* First, in France, we don't have coffee 'to go'. You drink it inside the coffee shop, because you can't really go anywhere with a coffee cup in your hand. We just

1 Mac versus PC

don't do that. And walking in flip-flops? *Oh non!* These are not shoes—not in the city. French girls have flip-flops, but only for the beach, come on! It would never cross a French girl's mind to put flip-flops on to walk around the city. No way. So, as I do these things it means I'm becoming American, right?

Claire stops by my apartment to get ready for Manayunk. Tonight I feel like anything is possible. I could meet *him*. My coworker Alison found her husband on the internet. Everyone knows at least one couple who met through an internet website. A singles party is kind of the same thing. It's a place where single people get together to try to find the person who will make their heart jump.

Manayunk is basically just one street—and all the bars and restaurants look alike. The village atmosphere, with lots of large terraces, is very attractive to French people. It's so hot in this city in the summer that it's hard to find outdoor spaces to have a drink. Everybody prefers to cool down in the air conditioning inside. But French people tend to enjoy having a drink outside, even if it's hot. So Manayunk is great for that.

Claire and I enter in the bar. First step: the girl at the entrance, who I'm pretty sure cannot possibly be single, smiles, takes our money, stamps our hands, and says: "the singles party is upstairs. Have fun!"

We go up. It's dark. I noticed that it's an American thing to dim the lights to make an event seem fancy. It definitely creates a romantic atmosphere in a good restaurant, but tonight I would prefer to see. How am I going to see *Him* in the dark? *Bref*, it's fine, I'm just overly motivated:

"I am excited to think that everyone here is single and looking for love!"

"Aurélie, you see the guy at the bar wearing sunglasses?

"*Oui*! He's cute!"

"Well, do you really think he is really looking for love, buying a beer for that redheaded girl?"

"You're cynical!" we laugh.

I finally make my way to the bar:

"Two Lagers, please!"

The bartender works out a lot. Without a doubt, he's dating the entrance girl. We say *'santé,'* cheers, and then Claire and I build our attack plan. She is pretty quick—already a cute guy targets her, and I end up alone before I can even finish my first Lager. I would have abandoned her too if I were in her shoes. I look around, evaluating my next move. I am surprised to see people of all different ages. I was expecting to see only young people. But no, the ages range from around thirty—which appears to be the average age of the women in the room—to about fifty. Everyone is surveying the crowd. I am not the youngest, either. I see a group of students from Drexel—it's written on their T-shirts. They are out of my age range, but they must be at least twenty-one, or they wouldn't have gotten in here.

"Hi! I'm Carl. You didn't come here to be alone!"

Lucky me, the guy who approaches me is really hot. Here we go!

"Hi! I'm Lilly. Nice to meet you!"

I smile and he takes a seat next to me:

"Nice atmosphere tonight! I live in center city, but I always enjoy coming to Manayunk."

"I live in Philly too." I say. "It's the first time I come to Manayunk."

"Where are you from, Lilly? I hear you have an accent...you're from Europe?"

"You're good!"

"Let me guess...Italian?"

"Close! I'm French!"

"That's cool! Paris is *'très joli.'* I've seen *Amélie* like a hundred times!"

At first it doesn't ring a bell, but then I realize he's talking about the movie *'Amélie Poulain.'* Why did the Americans cut *'Poulain'* from the title? Well, why do I care now? He seems willing to spend time with me:

"Another drink?" he says.

I follow him to the bar while trying to locate Claire in the crowd. I have no clue where she is. I check my cell. Nothing. We decided that we text each other if we leave with a guy. She must be some-where in the bar.

I focus on Carl. He is really friendly. He works for Microsoft. I tell him I plan on buying a new laptop, which is true. So he advises me on the different types. We were just beginning to flirt more obvi-ously when the barman makes an announcement. It's closing: 2 a. m. Carl isn't deterred:

"A last drink at my place?"

He is a little more ambitious than I am.

"*Oui*, I mean, I'll walk back to the train station with you, but maybe we can have another drink another day?"

"Sure! Can I get your number?"

Bien sûr, I give him my number but going to his place right away just doesn't feel right. We are walking to the train station when I get a text from Claire: "Nice work! Don't wait for me. I'm in good hands! ;-)" What a good night, Claire found a great guy too!

Carl and I kiss goodbye at Market East station.

"How do you feel about having brunch later?" he says.

"*Oui*! That's a good idea!" a brunch would be great.

"I'll call you when I wake up then. Sleep tight!"

Oui! If he wants to see me tomorrow even after I turned him down for tonight, he must really like me. I can't believe I met a potential future American boyfriend at a singles party! I'm anxious to see him for brunch and spend my day with him! Who would have thought?

*

At 11 a.m. I try to motivate myself to get up because when Carl calls for brunch I don't know how much time I'll have to get ready. I need to plan ahead. So when he calls, I'll just have to join him wherever he chooses! By noon, I'm as fresh and glamorous as a flower in a blue dress. It's already 31° C (88° F). Love July in Philly! At 1 p.m. I wonder what the common "brunch" time is in the U.S. I call Jenny to find out. She is excited for me:

"Tell me how was the single party!"

"Beyond expectation!" I say.

"Oh my God! You met someone?"

She wants all the details. I give her all the details.

"So here I am, wondering at what time he'll call for a brunch!"

"Usually we meet for brunch around 1 p.m."

She realizes it's 1:30 p.m. and adds:

"You know, Lilly, there's no 'right' time. You can have brunch any-time on the weekend. Until like 3 p.m.! You went to bed very late."

Oui, we went to bed very late. That makes sense. He is still sleeping and he'll call around 2 p.m.

I don't know if I should start painting my nails. What if he calls and my nails aren't dry yet? *Non*, that's not a good idea. Too compli-cated. I pick up a book, written in English. Miss McCarty would be so proud of me. Now I can read American books almost as fast as I read French ones. My cell rings. I leap to answer it—tossing my book aside. It's Claire. I answer…

She spent a wonderful night with Justin. I am happy for her, but right now she is keeping my phone line busy for nothing. Carl is going to call. I ask her if it would be ok to talk details tomorrow because I'm waiting on my own American guy call. She under-stands the emergency and we decide to talk tomorrow.

By 5 p.m. I'm ready to lose it. Why isn't he calling me? Why? At 6 p.m. I realize it's dinner time, so I take off my blue dress. Where did I go wrong? His last words were: 'I'll call you when I wake up.' Is he still sleeping? Did I dream these words?

*

Obviously on Monday I don't feel like having lunch with Claire. I spend my lunch break at the Apple store a few blocks away. Why not buy a Mac? A nice guy from the store arrives:

"Can I help you?"

"Thanks, I'm just having a look."

"The MacBook you're looking at is really cool. We have it in black too."

He's kind of cute, so if he really wants to give his little commercial speech, he can.

I invite him to continue:

"Yes I like it. But I'm French and I wonder if I could buy it with a French keyboard?"

I hate that we don't have the same keyboard, like we don't have the same system of measurement…why? Electronic devices are less expensive here but I don't want to be uncomfortable switching between the French and American keyboard. Is the price really worth the trouble?

"No… we don't sell foreign keyboards. But I can show you how to create shortcuts for your accented letters. You have accents, right? You'll see—It's really easy."

"Really?"

And he shows me. I explain our different accents and we joke around a bit. After 25 minutes of demonstration, I realize I have to hurry to get back to work.

"I'm Neil by the way!" he says. "Take my card. Feel free to come back anytime if you'd like an another demonstration."

Good salesman.

During the entire afternoon I stare at my phone hoping Carl calls. He could say: "I'm sorry about yesterday. I had to take care of my grandmother who needed a ride to the hospital / my dog died / my best friend was in trouble… but I felt a connection between us, and I want to see you again." But the silence harasses me. I call Jenny who says:

"I talked to Amy…"

"And?"

"She told me singles party is the new booty call place …"

"Ok, I've been in your country for a year and a half now and I have never heard about this type of call. What?"

"Oh. A booty call is when you call someone just to have sex…"

"I get it, but come on! Meeting people just to have sex at a singles party? Isn't it kind of implicit that people are not looking for that? Don't you go to clubs for that?"

Jenny and Amy are right. Apparently singles parties are the perfect places to meet a *boulet*. It's easy. And the girls think the guys are there with the same goal; otherwise they would be in some other bars… But no. The *boulet* just has to win them over for one evening… Carl just wanted me to spend the night? Ok… But when I refused, why did he propose brunch? It doesn't make any sense. I don't understand.

*

After much consideration, I eventually decide to buy a MacBook. I'll be able to write in French with an English keyboard. It didn't seem too hard to use the shortcuts. I can do it! Back to the Apple store, I look for Neil:
"Hi! I'm Lilly. I stopped by a week ago and I made my decision. I'd like to buy a MacBook."
"Sure Lilly! I remember you. *Bonjour!*" says Neil.
He goes to the back room and comes back with my computer. I realize this is a big investment. My old laptop is dying and losing my computer is like losing France to me! Without it I am alone in the world! No Skype and no Facebook: I'm cutoff from my family and my friends in France. I need this contact even with just a webcam. So I need this Mac.
"Come back any time, ok! I'd be happy to help you with your new laptop!" says Neil. Isn't he a great salesman? So, ok, he gets my number and he shows me a nice sleeve to protect my new acquisition.

3 days later I come back to ask him a few questions:
"Hi! Neil."
"Bonjour Lilly, how can I help you?"
"I do have a few questions since I turned on my new laptop…"
I smile and I take my notes. I had jotted down a list of questions as not to forget them in front of Neil. I would have looked silly.
"Thanks for helping me. It's for iTunes. You showed me how to get the album picture on the side. But I wasn't able to do it by myself, alone at home yesterday."
"No problem. I'll show you."
What an expert! We have a good time learning about my computer. For a while. Then I leave, thanking him so much.

I lose one more pound this week. The Weight Watchers woman congratulates me and offers me a bracelet. That's nice…when I think of it, with all the money I have already paid, it might as well be gold. But the applause is priceless. And my revenge on my body is priceless too. I am able to run –not fast obviously but still running- for an hour. The coach is very proud of me too. So is Philippe. And me: I love myself so much that sometimes I wonder if I really need someone else to love me too.

Bien sûr, if Neil is willing to add his love to mine I would let him. Third visit to the Apple store:
"Hi, Neil!"
"Hi, Lilly. I'm happy to see you! What's the matter?"
"I have another question."
"Sure, please have a seat."
He takes a Macbook from the display and we sit in our usual spot at the demonstration table. I grab my paper and attack:
"When I open Internet I'd like to see the Google page directly. How can I do that?"
"Ok! I'll do it with you step by step. First, open Safari."
I write down his explanations.
"Go to Preferences. Click on General. Home Page. Then enter the Google address. Done!"
"It seems so easy when you do it!"
We stand up and I walk through the door slowly as Neil says:
"You know that's actually the time to close so if you're free, we could have a drink?"
What a coincidence!
"*Oui*! Why not? It's happy hour!"
Our happy hour turns into dinner. Good! Neil works at the Apple store part time. He is a photographer. I appreciate his enthusiasm as he speaks about his passion. Really. But we talk a lot about photography and nothing else. It's a nice dinner, and he's a pleasant guy. Thanks to Yuriko, I can actually participate in the photography conversation. I act like I'm really into it. When the waiter comes with our desert, I tell him I'm having a good time but I don't feel

any of the "butterflies" I hear so much about. Honestly, I think I should give him Yuriko's number. Why am I not attracted to this guy? He seems nice, cute, fun. Well. The lack of attraction is mutual I guess because he says:

"Lilly! You do talk a lot, it's crazy!"

I laugh out loud in front of such an honest comment. I had the feeling that he was the one who has been delivering a monologue since we met. Weird... And he adds a joke - I hope it is:

"On top of that, English isn't even your native language! Man! You must really monopolize the conversation in French!"

Ok. If I gave him such a headache after only 3 hours, what will it be like after 30 years of marriage? He would kill himself. So ok. It doesn't seem like we should see each other again. I agree.

No hard feelings. We take off in separate directions after dinner. Back at home in front of my brand new laptop I hope that I won't have any big issues with it. There's no way I can beg for Neil's help anymore. Good job, Lilly!

From: LapetiteAurélieUSA
To: *"Poulettes"*
Subject: J-15 before your arrival

My *Poulettes*, you'll be here very soon! Yes!
I am so happy! It's hot here: 30°C, bring lots of light shirts and skirts. I see it's raining in Paris! You have a 20°C gap to handle!
I booked a room for us in New York. We can share a 2-bed room for the 4 of us. Perfect!
I'm sad Clémence can't join us. But it's such great news and a great excuse! 6 months pregnant already! I can't believe it… I feel like she broke the news yesterday!
I have everything planned: the tickets to go to the top of the Empire State Building for Julie, the boat tour of Manhattan for Manon, we have 4 seats for *Mamma Mia* on Broadway for Anaïs!
I'll pick you up at the airport Wednesday afternoon. Then we'll take a bus to New York on Saturday and come back on Tuesday. And you'll leave for Paris on Thursday. What a week is waiting for us!
Réviser votre anglais! Practice your English!
See you soon for real,
Aurélie, official New York guide

20. *Sex and the City, Version Française* [1]

"Aaaaaaaaaaaaaaah!" I yell in the airport.
"*Ma poulette!*" They yell back at me.
We are jumping up and down like we're kids on the first day of school after a long summer break. They are here, as promised. I want to share everything about my life here with them. Arriving at my place they are already amazed:
"Aurélie, you live on the 21st floor! So cool!"
I don't pay much attention to that now. It is unusual in France. The last floor would be the 6th maybe…buildings are smaller. We are so happy to be reunited that they are not tired at all. No jet lag. They are superwomen, *mes poulettes!*

I take them to Old City to have dinner at *Cuba Libre*. I love this place. The inside is decorated like a hacienda, with trees all around.
"I see at least 10 handsome guys in the restaurant. How can you still be single?" asks Julie.
"Come on'! It's not that simple… I met guys. Just not good ones…"
"Ok… But that's hard to believe! Look at the guy over there—he's cute! I already have my eyes on 5 guys I would love to get closer to…"
"So sad you don't speak English! Not even a word!" says Anaïs.
We laugh. I feel like it's easy to say 'this place is full of cute guys' …
The hard part isn't to meet someone –ok yes it is – but I did meet some guys. The hardest part is to meet a great guy you want to see again – and who wants to see you again too.

1 Sex and the city, French version

I prefer not to debate this because Julie would not understand anyway. Not everyone was lucky enough to meet their perfect match at 16 in high school. I decide to shift the attention to Anaïs:

"So Anaïs, tell me, how did moving in together go? How is it to live with your boyfriend?"

"We are so happy! It's crazy you've never met Antoine…"

"I know! Hopefully next time I'm in France I'll visit your sweet love nest!"

It feels weird to have missed an entire part of her life. I turn to Manon:

"So tell me the truth, how is he, this Antoine?"

"You remember the guitarist she dated in her first year of college?"

"Oh my god! I do! Why are you bringing up this *boulet* after all these years?"

"Well, same kind physically! Nicer personality but same idea!"

"No way!" says Anaïs.

"Way!" say Manon and Julie.

I believe them. Anaïs has always been attracted to the same guys. I would have been surprised if this one was completely the opposite.

"Now it's just you and me!" Manon says to me.

I clink glasses with her.

"Sometimes reading your emails, I really think you've found him! Your American boyfriend!" Says Manon. I wink, and she adds:

"I have to say I'm glad it didn't work out!"

Silence.

"Yeah…!" she says. "If you meet him you'll never come back! You'd stay here with him and we wouldn't see you anymore!"

"You're so sweet!" I say. "I love you girls."

*

The first hours with my friends are refreshing, and the next day I play tour guide. We stroll along and I show them Philadelphia. I make them taste the food specialty: the Philly cheese steak. And they comment on everything:

"People are really fat in this country!" Says Anaïs as we walk along

Walnut Street. I thank God that no one around understands what she is saying.

"I should have taken a extra jacket! Every time we enter a store it's freezing cold. What's the matter with them?" says Manon. They're not used to air conditioning. Summer isn't as hot in France and especially in Normandy, so we don't need it.

"Clothes are really cut in a weird way here! Nothing fits me here, it's weird! Where do you buy clothes?" says Julie.

"Oh! Look at that!" says Manon. "They have individual parking meters! Like we used to have!" She is so shocked that she takes a picture. In France, there's one ticket machine per block, not per parking space.

"Whoa. Did you see that?" She says. "That woman is wearing hospital scrubs outside?!"

"Yes, I see. There's a hospital right around the corner. What's the matter?"

"Aurélie, that's disgusting! A nurse wearing her work clothes outside? The streets are so dirty!"

Anaïs can't help but stare at every fat person she sees: "American women have no shame! I don't believe it. Look at this one—in France, a woman with those legs wouldn't dare go out wearing tiny shorts like those!"

"And what is that noise?" says Julie. An ambulance flies by.

"At first I was surprised too. They do make a lot of noise here, but eventually you just kind of learn to ignore it ..."

"Really? Why it is so loud? It's not that loud in France!"

I walk them to the Art Museum. We run up the stairs like in the Rocky movies. This is fun. Everyone takes a picture next to the Sylvester Stallone statue. They tell me they enjoy the view of the city—their first compliment. I'm exhausted so I propose a DVD night at the apartment with junk food. They want to try everything I told them about on my e-mails. Chicken wings that you eat with your fingers – so not French. Tortillas with many kinds of dips. A fried chicken basket from KFC. Some Chinese takeout. And all my favorites deserts—carrot cake and brownies. The best of the 'American cuisine.'

"Oh that's crazy!" says Anaïs from my kitchen. Worried, I join her. She's standing in front of my microwave.

"Is this a popcorn button? What is it?" she says.

She looks at me with empty eyes. I open the cupboard. Take a popcorn bag. Put it in the microwave and push the button. Anaïs is speechless.

A table! Dinner is ready! We sit around my table, where I have placed everything in the middle, which is strange for French people. I suggest that we avoid the normal French dinner order: *l'entrée*, the starter, then *le plat,* the main dish, *le fromage*, cheese, and then *le dessert*, desert. No! Tonight I put everything out we have and we will each go at our own rhythm.

"So! Tell us! Is it better here?" says Anaïs.

"Better?" the question surprises me. "No... It's different."

"Come on! You love living here!" says Julie.

"Yes I do. But I don't necessarily think it's better."

"So why don't you come back?"

"I'm working! I have a job here, remember? I signed a 2 year contract. I can't leave whenever I want!" I laugh.

"You said you'd come back after 6 months in Boston and then you moved to Philadelphia without coming back to France!"

"You know I love traveling. Is it so weird that I became an expatriate really?"

"Well, in high school you did take Greek lessons just because you knew they were planning a trip to Greece with the class."

"Exactly."

"I understand." Says Julie. "I think I'd like to live this kind of experience abroad."

"You talked about studying in Canada, didn't you?"

"Yes. I wanted to spend junior year in Canada. But Pierre didn't really want to move... I didn't want to leave him alone..."

"Oh you know! Everyday life is the same everywhere!" I say.

And what the hell, I admit it: "Ok yes, it's better here. I can get to New York in two hours whenever I want, and that's cool. I can watch shows that don't even exist in France yet. And I can get a manicure on any corner for $10! And now I speak fluent English!"

It's Saturday morning and we are on our way to New York! The 4 of us, sunglasses on, we are so ready to become Carrie Bradshaws. Our cameras are fully charged. The guidebook is in our hands. *Oui*, when I tell them I know the city by heart, I'm not kidding. Even in Paris I need a map...

The train drops us at Penn Station. A few blocks later we are crossing Times Square. My *Poulettes* get crazy because lights and sounds are coming from everywhere. I want to look like I'm used to it, so I say:

"Oh ladies, it's great, right? But it's even better when it's dark! We'll come back tonight!"

We check in at the hotel. Our room is on the 37th floor and we have a view over the Chrysler building. My friends are impressed. Mission accomplished! We get ready to go out into the streets of New York! On behalf of Amy, Jenny's BFF, I plan on going to The Marquee. *C'est la boite à la mode!* It's the most popular dance club right now, Amy told me.

"Showers are strange here! They haven't invented the flexible shower head yet?!" says Anaïs as she steps out of the bathroom.

"Come on!" I say. "Can't you stop complaining about silly things and just admire the view! For God's sake!"

I am a little confused by all their comments about stupid differences. We are in another country and on another continent, of course it's different! Don't we travel to learn new things?

My cell rings. Weird because Jenny and Claire know I'm in New York with my French friends so I have no clue who is calling me. Yuriko is back in Japan for 2 weeks. I don't recognize the number. It has to be a mistake so I don't pick up.

"Aurélie, answer it! So we can hear you speak English! It'll be fun! Miss bilingual!"

says Julie, giving me my cell.

Ok.

"Hi! This is Lilly!" I say with my best accent. The girls are all sitting around me on the bed.

"*Salut, Aurélie?*" answers a male French voice.

"*Oui?*"

My *Poulettes* are so disappointed to hear French that they leave me to finish their nails and makeup.

"It's Philippe, sorry to bother you."

"What's up?"

"Nothing! I ... Well... We worked a lot on this ad and, it's unusual that I am in Philly this weekend..."

"*Oui?*"

"I would like to invite you to a restaurant tonight, if you're free. To thank you for your work..."

"That's nice but I'm in New York for the weekend. I'm on vacation actually! I took 5 of my 10 days!"

"I didn't know, sorry... can I take a rain check on this one?"

"I'll be back to the office on Thursday, I give you a call."

"Let's do that! Enjoy your weekend..."

"I will! Bye!"

I hang up and then I realize my *poulettes* are back around me and they haven't missed a word of this quick and useless conversation... They have the 'tell me everything' look:

"What's going on?" I ask.

"Oh please, Aurélie! Who was he? Can we know?" says Anaïs, her eyes overflowing with curiosity.

"You mean on the phone?!" I say.

"Yes! Who was that?" says Julie. She only has makeup on one eye, and it gives her a strange gaze. It feels like Cruella Deville is interrogating me...

"That was nobody! Philippe, a French colleague."

"A nobody who asked you to have dinner with him?" says Manon.

"*Oui* but it's nothing like that." I say, beginning to understand where they are going with their questioning.

"And what does he look like, this Philipp nobody?" says Anaïs.

"*Non!* It's not like that I swear!" I say.

"This male colleague calls you to ask you out...it's not very professional!" Says Manon.

"Ok, I'll stop you right there. He's gay!" I say.

"And you really think we're going to buy that excuse!"

"I'm telling you! I know that from another French colleague. And in any case he's out as a potential match—he's much older!"

"Old? What does that mean? Bullshit!" says Manon.

"You're getting it wrong. This guy is never in Philly. He must be stuck tonight and I'm the only person he knows in the area, nothing crazy underneath..."

End of the story. My *poulettes* are disappointed, but I don't let them talk about it much: tonight, New York belongs to us!

Manon is the one who wants to put out her hand to hail a yellow cab. We arrive in Chelsea, in front of the club, Le Marquee. God the line is so long... Standing in our heels we have a lot of fun analyzing everyone else's look. The line here is so different from Parisian ones. Here, girls dress up. Beautiful dresses, beautiful colors! Different styles! Even at a popular club, the American girls wear very updated styles and it seems to work for them, well most of the time! We laugh until we hear another group speaking French. That happens a lot in New York, but not that much in Philly, so I'm used to not paying attention when I say stupid things with Claire. But in New York, there are so many French people... I always tell myself I should be more careful... So we turn lower our voices ... We're still in line... The bouncer, built like a tank of course, looks at us. He checks us out without even trying not to be obvious... Anaïs is the clear winner! He obviously finds her the most attractive in our group:

"Hi! Where are you girls from? You're all together?"

Anaïs smiles and I speak:

"Yes! We're all together! We're from Paris!"

"Well, come on in, Frenchies!"

He lets us in and replaces the velvet rope right behind us. Thanks, Anaïs! We dance for the rest of the night! It has been so long since we spent a girls' night out like that!

At 4 a.m., we're back at Times Square and they agree with me:

"It's crazier than it was this afternoon! I think there are even more people!" yells Julie. A pedicab offers us a ride, but Manon prefers to hail a cab. With 4 girls in heels, a car is more convenient.

4 hours of sleep later, we are not totally awake as we enter a Harlem church at 9 a.m., cheerful gospels gracefully opening our eyes.

When we arrive at Central Park and Fifth Avenue, our enthusiasm is back:

"Look! This is the Tiffany boutique from the movie *Breakfast at Tiffany's*!" shouts Anaïs, wriggling her ring finger.

"What is going on here?" says Manon. 'What are all these people waiting for?"

"I think they're waiting to enter in this store? Is that even possible?" I am not sure.

"Let's cross the street!" says Manon. And they cross the street where they stand, not bothering to take the walkway. This is the Parisian way, crossing anywhere! It worries me.

There is indeed a huge line to enter in this store. We go to have a look inside.

"Oh my God!" says Manon. "We have to do it! Let's get in line!"

I am on my tippy toes. I try to see what motivates them. Being short is frustrating.

"There's a shirtless guy!' says Anaïs. "He is at the entrance and a blond girl takes your picture with him!"

"We need our picture with the American naked guy!" says Manon.

"I don't see anything! There're so many people! Is he really naked?" I say.

We almost fight to decide which one will pose next to the half naked model. He wears jeans, buttons open. Manon and I are the two single ones, so we have the advantage. The blond photographer is nice enough to take four pictures so we all have proof that we touched an American guy.

"It's crazy! Too bad we don't have a store like that on *les Champs Elysées*!" says Anaïs.

"Don't worry!" I say. "I heard they have one in London already and that the next store will be in Paris!"

"Well, poor guy, the weather isn't that nice in London or Paris!" she says.

We walk down to the library then decide to go back to the hotel before dinner. Tonight we have a Broadway show. *Mamma Mia!* Sequins and disco music! Yes!

Nothing is better than a picnic in Central Park on a sunny day. We have a blanket (from the hotel) and enjoy our sleepy mood. *Une petite faim?* Something to eat? There's food everywhere! There are snack carts all around the park. Hot dogs, pretzels, New York specialties! Manon does her 'Manon thing,' refusing to eat from anything that isn't fixed in one place... Go figure!

A digestive stroll takes us to the Strawberry fields; this John Lennon commemorative site is very famous in Europe. And it's time to leave this peaceful outdoorsy place and reenter the city and head to the Empire state building. We are on the top of the building for the sunset: it's worth the wait. We are speechless, looking at the New York skyline. Heights aren't even measured on the same scale in France. Hovering above New York City is breathtaking for someone who grew up in a flat land. Everything is just so perfect at this moment when the two poulettes with boyfriends dare to break the silence: "It's so beautiful! I wish my other half were here to share this!" Manon and I communicate with a single look.

*

Tuesday, our last day in the Big Apple. We begin with the circle line tour, then we walk to Ground Zero. From there, we take the subway to Chambers Station, near city hall. I love this little park with its cute fountain. After the garden, we decide to walk on the Brooklyn bridge that begins right here. We don't go all the way because our feet start to hurt pretty badly. We don't want to miss the New York Stock Exchange. We're having so much fun taking obscene photos with the Bull! It begins when I tell them that touching the intimate parts of the bull brings you fortune and luck! Oh well! I am ashamed when a bus full of Japanese tourists stops in front of the statue to take a picture. I really hope they don't realize that we are French.

My *poulettes* are exhausted on the bus, leaving New York with plenty of unforgettable memories. Sometimes I wonder if a guy will be able to make me feel as good as I do in these moments with my girlfriends…even if deep inside me I wish one day I'll enjoy these moments as a couple.

They leave the U.S. very happy. They love Philly and New York. At least they tell me so. And they wish me luck in my search for my American boyfriend.

From: LapetiteAurélieUSA
To: "*Poulettes*"
Subject: *Vous me manquez déjà*! I already miss you!

Hi! My chicks (I guess you can translate *poulette* like that?!)
This week with you was amazing ;-) What an empty feeling I had
when I came back from the airport...
We'll put our pictures on Facebook as soon as possible, ok?
I hope you had a good flight back and that you slept. In this way,
the time difference is less difficult.

Back at work I feel miserable...I need to sleep! And I went for a
run: what a mistake! Too much walking, hot dogs, and alcohol??!!!)

Look at the picture of us on the boat with the Statue of the Liberty
in the background, aren't we so cute?
XOXO,

Aurélie,

21. *Un baiser 'à la française'* [1]

Nous y sommes ! Here we go! I am 26. Still single. Several extra pounds. "What have I accomplished this year?" I ask myself as I lay in bed, reflecting. I don't like birthdays. Jenny and Claire wanted to throw a party for me, but I declined and negotiated a small birthday dinner instead.

It's the end of my first year with P.A.J. Industries. My HR manager has already asked to meet with me. What should I do? I'm not required to sign on for another year. I remember how excited I was when I arrived in the U.S.—marveling at school buses, taking photos of taxis, seeing squirrels for the first time in Boston Common. Today I hate school buses—they slow down traffic—and I've discovered that squirrels are devilish little animals that fearlessly saunter up to my blanket to steal pieces of my muffin as I lay on the grass. They scare me. And I just spent $10 on a wedge of camembert, my favorite cheese, from Normandy—twice the price I would have paid in France.

On the other hand, if I don't renew my contract, I'll never meet my American boyfriend. It's been 2 years...and nothing. Why is this happening to me? Men are just too complicated and American guys don't seem any easier to understand than French men. Too bad...

Claire is happy to be headed back to France at the end of the year. At least she had a little American romance—he wasn't the man of her life, but at least she had an American boyfriend. And Jenny can't stop talking about her wedding and, as if that weren't enough, my coworkers are driving me crazy with their "Lilly, can you come here a minute?" "Lilly, are you done yet?" "Lilly, blah blah blah." I can't take it anymore—I miss being Aurélie!

---

1 French kiss

As soon as I get to work in the morning, I see a Post-it on my computer. "Lilly - come see me first thing please.-Bob."

My boss has never left me such a message, so I'm curious. I head to his office and knock on the door as Alison in the office next door shouts:

"Lilly! There you are. Bob is looking for you."

I'm only 20 minutes late. Alison says:

"He'd like you to join him in the CEO's office, ok?"

I have never been to the CEO's office before. Alison doesn't give any more information and goes back to snacking. It's 9:30 a.m.

I grab a pen and notebook, as well as my pass to enter the top floor, and walk to the elevators. At the 40th floor reception, a pretty admin escorts me to the CEO's office and opens the door. A gorgeous view of the city immediately catches my eye and then I notice a sofa, a coffee table, a huge desk, and a conference table with four people sitting around it. Bob stands and joins me at the door:

"Lilly! Great! Come here."

"Bonjour!"

I decided to say "bonjour" to everyone from now on. That way, hopefully some of the people I run into will know at least one French word. Surprised, the three other men turn their heads and look at me. Bob introduces me:

"Let me introduce you to Lilly, a French communications specialist who joined my department a year ago."

The three men turn their heads back to their papers and continue talking. Bob explains:

"We have a problem I hope you can help us with."

"What's going on?"

"We're working on a global ad project. By global, I mean that we're developing one ad for everywhere in the world, and we'll just translate the text, ok?"

"Ok."

"Please have a seat and take a look at the draft the Parisian team sent us."

I see a beautiful, green park, full of light. At the foreground is a couple, sitting on a bench, stealing a kiss. It's a lovely photo. I look

158

at Bob, confused as to what he requires my help with.

"Very nice—they linked the themes of green, love, and chemistry very well! And I see that it's already been translated into English, so what can I do for you?"

The CEO and the two other men stare at me, shocked. And Bob says:

"Nothing in this picture catches your eye or bothers you?"

"No…"

Is this a trick question? I'm lost. Doesn't the CEO have something more important to do? Bob breaks the silence:

"I told you. It's just a cultural misunderstanding."

When an American person says 'it's just a cultural misunderstanding,' it means there's a problem. So I ask:

"Where is the cultural misunderstanding?"

"They're making out!" says Bob.

"And?" I ask.

For the first time, Bob speaks to me in a paternal voice:

"We can't run an ad in an American industrial magazine with two people French kissing. It's inappropriate!"

Ha! I'm completely blown away by this uniquely Anglo viewpoint. And this is how I found myself explaining to the CEO of a multinational corporation that, in France, a photo of people kissing isn't shocking at all—even in an advertisement, even in the industrial world. Today, I really earned my salary.

From: LapetiteAurélieUSA
To: *"Poulettes"*
Subject: *Vive la France!*

Hi! My *Poulettes*!

Ever since your visit, I've been wondering if I should stay in the U.S. or return to France.

I've been compensating for my lack of American boyfriend by running 3 times a week. My coach is my new best friend. The half marathon is in one month and I'm not even scared. I'm so excited! I love it, and I happily read Runner magazine every month. Do you know there's a fashion season for sports clothes?
At first, I came to the U.S. to meet a guy, but even though there's no one to flirt with me at the moment, I'm still going.

At least I fell in love with an American hobby lol…

Bisous, kisses,
Aurélie, runs with no goal.

22. *Tout le monde va de l'avant* [1]

Jenny sends me a weird e-mail saying she has good news. What's going on with her? She is going to tie the knot. I already know that. Is she pregnant? I would be really surprised if she were, because she is so focused on being a beautiful bride that she hired a home personal trainer twice a week. She can't be pregnant. So what is it?

We agree to have dinner at 7 p.m., and Jenny is nice to eat kind of late for her because she knows I never adapted to the 6 p.m. American dinnertime. Sorry, but there's no way. Even if I stay longer, I don't think I will be able to eat that early!

Cuba Libre restaurant: we have a drink, a passion fruit mojito, and I feel better. Also, it proves that she's not pregnant. It's Saturday, so we admire the professional salsa dancers.

"Jenny, it's amazing how much weight you've lost!"

She does look thin. Is it the wedding effect? I pull my top down over my butt. Our table is ready. We sit.

"Thank you, Lilly! You lost weight too, didn't you?"

"You're nice. I do run a lot nowadays. But I haven't lost like you did!"

I describe my training schedule and goals for the half marathon. I'm really excited to tell her about my new hobby. Jenny takes the opportunity to tell me her news:

"Unfortunately Lilly I won't be able to wait for you at the finish line…"

"Oh, don't worry! I understand—it's a Sunday morning. If I weren't running it myself, I would never get up that early on a Sunday morning!"

1 Everyone moves on

She takes my hands and looks me in the eye:

"I won't be able to come because I won't be living in Philly anymore…"

She sees that I don't understand, so she rephrases:

"My honey found a job in San Francisco. We're moving back home!"

What? Jenny is leaving? I always thought that I would be the one to leave first.

"Oh, Jenny! I am happy for you…"

"I know… but I'll miss you."

"*Oui*! I'll miss you too!"

A little tear comes to my left eye. Jenny explains:

"You know our families are in California."

"*Oh oui?…*"

"And of course it will be so much easier to plan the wedding!"

"Of course! I am happy for you. But when do you have to leave?"

"In 2 weeks."

"*Quoi*? What? From Philly to San Francisco? In 2 weeks? Is that even possible!"

"Yeah—funny how fast life changes, right?"

I am happy for them. But she is my best American friend… Her friendship means so much to me. I'm proud to be her French friend. And for me, having an American *poulette* is rather unusual, and I love it! I am going to miss her.

*

I wake up, it's 10:30 a.m. Oops! I slept through Sunday morning training with the group. I've noticed that mojitos decrease the chance that I will be able to run a 16k the following morning. I'll remember that. Just four weeks to go before the big race. Missing the training is not a smart move. We all follow the Runner magazine training program. This morning was an important step in the process…

At work they haven't recovered from the 'French kiss ad' incident yet. They make me call the French Communications director to explain why this ad will not work in the U.S. On top of this mess, Philippe asks for a lot of work on a new project.

And I receive an e-mail from Yuriko that could easily fill a novel. I haven't had news from her in awhile, so I'm excited to read it. Last time I heard from her was in May, and she sent me pictures of her graduation party. She is a photographer now, and she spent the summer traveling around the U.S. to create her portfolio. She took wonderful shots of the desert. She is so talented. She is now ready to jump into the business. She made her choice: she is going back to Japan to begin her career. She already has contacts to exhibit her photographs in an art gallery there, and she invited me to visit her country anytime. She apologized for not having time to stop by Philly and say goodbye, but promised to keep in touch. We'll see each other soon, we know it. Everything turned out so well and so fast for her.

Claire returns to France in three months to finish school, Jenny moves back to California next weekend, and now Yuriko is going back home too. They've all made up their minds. They know where they are going. And what about me?
I have to get motivated because I am supposed to run 21 km in 3 weeks. American boyfriend or not at the finish line, I have to make it through...
Instead of going to training this week I decide to customize my sports gear! When you're stressed, sometimes you need to do silly things. I also just learned, from TV, that my American name, Lilly, is a flower's name. Almost. Like in 'Lily of the valley'. I can't explain it but I feel I need to do some decorating and add these flowers everywhere. I can run and sweat, but still remain fashionable. I'll be the cutest runner of the race. Why do I worry so much about being single, really?

*

This morning, I try to remain focused, with *Don't Worry Be Happy* playing on my iPod. I go straight to work. With my gym bag on my back, nothing can stop me. Nothing can stop a motivated woman, except a *boulet, bien sûr…* I run into Philippe who waves at me from across the street at 15th and Market.

"Bonjour Aurélie."

"Bonjour…"

"Ready for the half marathon? It's on Sunday, isn't it?"

"Yeah…it's on Sunday. I hope I'll finish it. It's my first race, you know. I'm a bit anxious…"

"You'll do it! You've been following the training!"

"I did miss a few trainings…"

"When I was training for the New York Marathon, I couldn't make myself available for all the training sessions either but you'll see it's ok!"

"What was your time?"

"4h02!"

"Wahoo! You're good…"

"Thank you, but it's not the time that maters really. The goal for a first race is to cross the finish line … still running."

"Obviously… And are you going to run it too?"

"No. Unfortunately I leave tonight for work in Asia. Be back in a week."

"That's cool!"

"Well… This kind of trip is more exhausting than cool. I just visit chemical plants."

"Oh, ok." I'm thinking how irritating it is that this guy always seems to see the glass half empty, when I notice him checking me out as I get out of the elevator! Thomas can think what he wants, but I've never received this kind of look from a gay man.

*

The Friday before the race my colleagues stop by my cubicle to wish me luck. Each of them has advice for me! Bob remains confused—he's not an athletic person and doesn't really understand my interest. Still, he says he hopes I'll make it to work on Monday.

I can't believe I'm awake on a Sunday morning at 6 a.m., waiting at the starting line of the Philadelphia half marathon. I'm transfixed by the music, the swarming crowd, and the rainbow of colors represented in the runners' gear. The crowd isn't as dense as it was for the 4th of July fireworks, but almost. I'm being pushed from every side. We're like ants on an anthill. Some groups are formed based on the time runners think they'll finish. I keep moving to the back. I'm happy that it's crowded, because it's freaking cold in November in Philly. Eventually, I find the P.A.J. Industries team. I zigzag through the crowd to reach them. Some are kind of surprised to see me, having missed so much of the training. Ok here we go! I'm wearing my belt, with small bottle of orange juice and honey attached. I'm in my best running clothes, with the lilies on them. And, for a glamorous touch, I'm wearing the Nike earrings I saw in Runner magazine. I feel great as huge speakers blast music from the movie *Rocky*. Haven't I become such an American girl? Let's go!

The entire crowd starts to run in one big wave! I find that it's best to follow the flow. Otherwise, I'm afraid I'll be trampled. The race snakes all over town. On the sidewalks, supporters play music, hang posters, drink warm coffee, and eat donuts. They wear hats and scarves, and I'm jealous. Why did I decide to do this again?
I've already lost the other members of my team, but I'm still running. 10 km. There are runners behind me. I'm surprised I'm not the last one. 15 km. I'm so tired, I feel like my tongue is dragging on the ground. When we finally make it to the banks of the Schuylkill River, I am reenergized when I see the "Three Fairies" statue we passed so often in training. From this point, I know it takes me only 30 minutes to get to the finish line.
I've been running for 1 hour 43 minutes…the last 30 are the worst. It's all flat. I focus. It's hard, but I can't stop now! I'm amazed to think that the finish line is still only the halfway point for people who run full marathons.

2h14! I eventually cross the line! I hear people applauding and cheering me! I did it! I have never felt so proud of myself, and they place a medal around my neck. The rest of the team waited for me, how sweet! They all finished half an hour ago, but they stuck around to congratulate me.

There's no American boyfriend to tell me how great I am, but I don't care. Really. My own happiness is enough to fulfill me!

I spend the rest of the day in bed, my medal still around my neck, eating a huge carrot cake I hid in my fridge for the occasion. My cell rings, it's a text from Philippe:

"Bravo! Repose-toi bien." (Congrats! Rest up.)

*

Monday, it's back to work. My medal around my neck, I am not concentrating. I just want everyone to see my medal. Claire laughs out of loud. I don't care—I ran 21 km! Now I am strong enough to face my HR manager:

"I'd like to stay one more year. Thank you for the opportunity! Where do I sign?"

"Great. I heard you were really helpful on a global project."

I smile, thinking of the French couple kissing on the bench. I can't help it.

From: LapetiteAurélieUSA
To: *"Poulettes"*
Subject: *I did it!*

Mes poulettes, you're going to be proud of me!

Look at the picture of my medal. I ran the Philadelphia half marathon in 2 hours and 14 minutes. I gave everything I could! I loved it. Not in the moment, of course. But after. Next year I'll run the entire marathon!

And big news: I made up my mind. My life is a mess here but I like that way. Even alone! So I signed for one more year at work.
My friends Claire, Jenny, and Yuriko are all leaving and going back home… I know that it will be different, but I feel I have to stay.

I'll be back for Christmas to renew my visa. Let's meet on the 26th in Paris on the Champs Elysées like always for our Christmas celebration!
Merci les filles!
Maybe you can visit me again next year?

Aurélie, loving the American single life

23. *C'est lui l'homme de ma vie? Non!* [1]

I am at my desk at work, booking my flight to Paris to renew my visa at the American embassy when Philippe pops his head into my cubicle. He always picks the perfect time to show up. He sits and says:

"So how did it go?"

"Excuse me?"

"The half marathon?"

"Oh! Good! 2h14!"

"*Félicitations*, congrats!"

"Thank you!"

"Are you sore all over?"

"It was hard to get up at the beginning of the week, but now I feel better."

"How was the race atmosphere?"

"Amazing! People playing music, a big crowd on the Parkway, huge!"

"It's always very friendly!"

"And how was your trip to Asia?"

"It was ok."

"Ok…"

"I'll be in the city this weekend, would you like to have a drink to celebrate your race?"

What should I answer? He might be waiting for an excuse, but I wonder why I shouldn't say yes. I won't be hunting for guys this weekend anyway, so why not have a drink with this colleague? The time I take to think is probably impolite because he feels he has to justify his invitation:

1 He is the man of my life ? No way !

169

"You can invite your friends! I don't know a lot of people here, so I'd enjoy meeting your friends!"

I am silly. This guy clearly just wants to get out of his apartment and not to alone all weekend. And what about me? I have a date with my TV!

"I'd love to have a drink! Tomorrow night? Where would you like to go?"

His face shows his surprise at my unexpected enthusiasm:

"I walk past this French place, Le Caribou, on my way to work every morning. I'd like to try it."

"Good idea! I've never been there! And I am desperately looking for a place where they serve *kir*! Maybe they do?"

"Ok! We'll see! Sounds like a plan!"

"*Oui*! See you!"

Why did I just say 'see you' in a teenage voice, and in English? Anyway… I call Claire to ask her to join us but she can't make it. Her whole weekend is booked before her departure. It's hard to say, but I don't know who else I can call… so I'll go alone. Too bad for him if he was hoping to meet my girlfriends!

*

The next day, I'm standing on the corner of 12th and Chestnut in front of Caribou. It's 7:30 p.m. on the dot. It looks warm and cozy inside. I'd like to go in because I'm freezing outside. I bet the temperature is negative in Celsius. Isn't it rude to make a girl wait outside in this weather? I think I've been nice enough to agree to leave my apartment on a Saturday to meet a coworker. The least he can do is to be on time, right? 7:41—I can't feel my toes anymore. Why did I wear heeled leather boots instead of my UGGs? At 7:50, he arrives with a big smile:

"Why are you waiting outside in this cold?"

"Hey! You're 20 minutes late!"

"We said 19h30/20h00. I'm on time… in the French sense!"

"I've been here since 19h30."

"I see…American time." He jokes.

"I've been living here for 2 years, maybe I can't adjust back! I think it's a good thing to be on time, actually. I prefer the American method."

"I'll remember that."

He looks at me genuinely surprised, as I reflect on the situation. Well, now we're here. I just want to have a drink and go back to sleeping, wrapped in my comforter. French guys aren't gentlemen—I forgot this detail.

We sit, and he takes a look at the menu. Relieved, he says:

"They do have your favorite aperitif, un *kir*!"

"I can't believe it, you found the only place in Philly where they serve them."

I receive this news with an exaggerated enthusiasm, but I do miss this drink. Every single bar and small restaurant in France serves this drink. I am surprised it truly does not exist the U.S. It's so simple: red berry liquor and white wine. With champagne instead of wine, it becomes a '*kir royal*' The ironic thing is, I almost never order a *kir* in my country, too basic! It's strange to be craving one lately.

"A *kir* and a flute of champagne, please!" Philippe orders, and I forgive him being late.

The waiter brings our drinks and I find myself thinking that, from a certain angle, Philippe looks quite handsome—swapping his 80s wardrobe for a few things from the Abercrombie catalogue.

He tells me about China, where he lived for three years, when he was my age, he adds. I catch the occasion to ask how old he is: 32! No way! *Oops*! I realize that Claire and I were way off—it's just that he doesn't have a very youthful aura.

"Would you like another drink?" he says.

"Sure."

The waiter comes with a second round. Philippe has visited all of Asia. He shows me pictures from his iPad. He has a lot of entertaining anecdotes, and we laugh a lot. My turn, so I tell him about the year I spent in Boston, the places I've traveled in the U.S.—San Francisco, Las Vegas... He tells me about Beijing, Singapore... I don't know Asia, and he doesn't know the U.S., except Philly, but he hasn't even visited the Liberty Bell yet, so I'm not sure I can even say that he knows the city.

By the third round, we're debating the similarities and differences between American and French culture.

"I'm hungry, would you like to eat something?" he asks.

I'm hungry too. Three kirs without peanuts—the typical snack they serve with the aperitif in French bars—and my head is spinning! The waiter offers us a table upstairs to eat. Philippe is kind of talkative, even when not speaking about glue. And I don't want to get the wrong idea, but some of the things he says, and the way he looks at me, I'm starting to think he might be flirting with me… Is it flirting, or is it just the alcohol? I mean, hypothetically, is it even possible? Because, based on our conversation, he's not gay and he not my dad's age, so he is definitely in the 'potential boyfriend' category. Except the fact that he's not American—just French. But hey, does it really matter anymore? And the most important characteristic on my *'boulet* avoidance checklist' is, "is he single"? Men are all available. But I mean, is he single. I have to find out:

"By the way, what happen to your girlfriend? Did she find a great apartment?"

"Who?"

"Remember I gave you a website to look for an apartment for your girlfriend who was moving to town?"

"Oh! Sure, my friend Hélène! But she's not my girlfriend! It's crazy you thought that. With my travels and everything… It's not easy to meet someone so I don't have a girlfriend…"

"Oh, I didn't understand."

"That's ok! She's a friend from my college years. She moved to Philly with her husband and their 18 months old daughter. They did find a great place, thank you!"

"How did they find it?"

"Thanks to the French community! They joined *'Philadelphia Accueil'* the French expatriate association of Philly. They found help right away!"

"I've heard of it."

"There are a lot of French people here—it's scary!"

I try to sort my thoughts as I laugh. He loves travelling, he is active, and he could be cute (with a wardrobe makeover). A chill goes down my spine. Wait a second. If he is 32 and still single, there must be something wrong with him. He must be a *boulet* in some way.

"Aurélie, you said you're from Normandy, right?"

"*Oui*! I'm from Rouen."

"No kidding!"

No one has ever been that excited to hear that I am from Rouen.

"No joke. Born and raised in Rouen."

"Me too! I went to Corneille high school, downtown." He says.

"No way! I went there too!"

There are some extraordinary coincidences that one cannot ignore. I wonder how I could have missed for months the wonderful potential I see in this guy.

We share some high school memories. He was several years ahead of me, so we never met, but we did share some teachers. Like the tiny English teacher with curly blond hair, who always wore an electric blue suit. She hated me, and he doesn't remember her fondly, either. He was as bad as I was in English! She would lose her mind hearing us speak better English than her now, living in the U.S.

We both couldn't believe it—when the waiter takes our plates away, Philippe confides:

"I'm full—that was delicious. But I've got a major flaw, I can't resist chocolate! Would you share a desert with me?"

I must be dreaming.

"The double chocolate cheesecake?" I answer instantaneously.

"Perfect choice!"

I officially want to kiss him. We could have gone on talking for hours, but the waiter eventually comes over and announces:

"We're closing! It's 2 a.m. guys!"

Philippe and I look at our watches by reflex. It is indeed 2 a.m. We look deeply at each other. We both have a smile on our lips without meaning to. We put on our coats and we are now standing on the sidewalk under the Le Caribou sign. At this moment, I realize I

173

don't want to let him go. I feel I'm looking at him for the first time. How could I have missed this all this time?

We stand there for a while. We don't talk; my eyes get lost in his. The cold eventually pushes us to move, and I put my arm under his as we walk slowly to my place. I feel like he is just as anxious as I am. I'd like to ask him to come up, but at the same time I'm not ready. I'm still kind of in shock. Yesterday, Philippe was still in my 'not even possible' category. I would give anything to know if he feels like I do now. Is he as surprised as I am by this feeling? Am I over-thinking the whole thing?

"I've had the most wonderful time tonight. I've been wanting to ask you out for awhile."

"Oh! I had a wonderful time too."

"I had never thought I would meet someone as amazing as you. It's so unexpected."

"I feel the same way! So unexpected."

It's really cold, but I'm boiling on the inside. I want to take off my gloves, my hat, my scarf, and my coat and… *Non*! Philippe must be in the same state as me. His cheeks are red but not from cold. He is just so adorable wearing his *Eagles* hat, like an American…but with something else that makes him more attractive than any American I've met.

Our breath freezes around us, and we laugh. I can't take my eyes off of his. We get closer. He gently presses his lips on mine, and our noses bang together. By reflex, I push him back and I cover my nose with my glove. We laugh. But I won't let it ruin our first kill. I wrap my hands around his neck and kiss him for real. He responds with an even longer and warmer kiss.

From: LapetiteAurélieUSA
To: *"Poulettes"*
Subject: *Je l'ai trouvé !* I found him!

My beloved poulettes,

Yeaaaah! This is both exciting and scary—I think I met the man of my life. It's Philippe! Seriously! We are still in a state of shock.
Everything I thought I knew about him was wrong. Philippe is 32 and he is from Rouen! Anaïs, he went to Corneille high school like us! I know, it's crazy, lol!
He is so sweet, and I love being around him.
It has been three weeks and we can't get enough of each other. I didn't tell you right away because I wasn't sure... Don't be mad! That's why I disappeared!
We will come back to Paris together for Christmas break on the 22nd.
Hoping you'll forgive me for keeping him a secret for so long, I asked him to join us on the 26th so you can meet him!
I'm coming back home with *mon petit ami!*
I eventually found my American boyfriend lol. Well, French boyfriend in America, but that counts for something! Even if it's not what I originally had in mind...

Love u,
Aurélie, in a relationship for real

24. *Il se marièrent et eurent beaucoup d'enfants* [1]

One year later.

I hear the keys turning in the door. It's Philippe. He's just getting home from work: it's 7 p.m. He never got into the American rhythm! Me, I leave at 5:30 p.m. like everyone else. Leaving work at 7 p.m. is so French! But it's ok. Working at the same place as your boyfriend isn't easy to handle discretely, so it's better to maintain different work schedules.

"Hi! *Mon amour*! I'm so happy." He says, kissing me.

"These flowers are so beautiful, you didn't have to!"

"You're kidding! You've signed another year contract just to stay here with me. Let's celebrate!"

"It was not even conceivable for me to leave you here. I want to stay with you. But I'm happy to celebrate! What about making reservation at Le Caribou this week-end?"

"I have a better idea." He smiles. "Would you like to spend the weekend in New York?"

"Oh! Philippe! That's a great idea! We live so close and we never go! And with the Christmas decorations it will be wonderful! Let's book a hotel tonight before you change your mind!"

"I've already made arrangements."

"Merci!"

"Friday night, we'll see The Phantom of the Opera on Broadway."

"Oh! That's so romantic!"

"And for Saturday evening, I was thinking we should go to a French restaurant, what do you think?"

"You seem to have some great ideas for this weekend, so please organize anything you'd like!"

---

1 And they lived happily ever after

From: LapetiteAurélieUSA
To: *"Poulettes"*
Subject: *New York, New York!*

My *poulettes*,
It was a magnificent weekend in New York. I enjoyed everything at a beautiful French restaurant.
When the waiter arrived with our desserts and announced, before presenting mine:
"And this is the chocolate cake."
And he put in front of me a plate covered by a silver dome. He opened it quickly. And there it was.
At first I didn't get it. I turned my head to Philippe and said:
"Oh! We don't have the same."
On his plate was the most wonderful-smelling chocolate cake. On my plate was a blue box. 'It's not my birthday,' I thought.
I began to open it, and I looked at him. It's at this moment that I understood. Something in his eyes. *Oh mon Dieu!* I couldn't open it anymore. I gave it to him saying:
"Do it, I can't!"
I began to cry, my heart beating faster and faster. I was so happy that I couldn't say anything. My voice was completely gone. The restaurant felt very hot. "Wait," I shouted and took off my coat. I wiped away my tears so I could see him. He just smiled, nervously. And I think I was smiling so much that it is impossible for me to show more teeth.
"Will you marry me?" he said.
I wanted to say yes, but I was crying… Well, I was trying to avoid crying, which is ten times harder. Finally, I screamed:
"Oui Oui Oui Oui Oui!" I couldn't stop saying, *"Oui Oui Oui…"*

We kissed and laughed. It was the best feeling ever. When we came back down from heaven, we realized, under the applause of the waiters, that we were the last customers in the restaurant.

Love you all,
Aurélie, *future mariée,* bride to be

The end.

Acknowledgments:

To Jaclyn, my American best friend. Without her help it would not have been the same. I'm so thankful to her. Merci for all the work she did on my English translation and for all the encouragement she provided in bringing this project to life.
To Céline, my daughter's godmother.
To my parents, my brother and all my family and friends who encourage me every day.
To all of you who read this book.
Special thanks to Patricia Galoisy, my publisher, who made my dream come true.

www.ingramcontent.com/pod-product-compliance
Lightning Source LLC
Chambersburg PA
CBHW030035030726
47500CB00001B/119